THE
SECRET
LIFE OF
WRITERS

GUILLAUME MUSSO

TRANSLATED FROM THE FRENCH
BY VINEET LAL

W&N
WEIDENFELD & NICOLSON

First published in Great Britain in 2021 by Weidenfeld & Nicolson,
This paperback edition first published in Great Britain in 2022
by Weidenfeld & Nicolson,
an imprint of The Orion Publishing Group Ltd
Carmelite House, 50 Victoria Embankment
London EC4Y 0DZ

An Hachette UK Company

First published in French as *La vie secrète des écrivains* by Calmann-Lévy.

1 3 5 7 9 10 8 6 4 2

A CIP catalogue record for this book is
available from the British Library.

ISBN (Mass Market Paperback) 978 1 4746 1914 1
ISBN (eBook) 978 1 4746 1915 8
ISBN (Audio) 978 1 4746 1947 9

Typeset by Input Data Services Ltd, Somerset

Printed and bound in Great Britain by Clays Ltd, Elcograf S.p.A.

MIX
Paper from
responsible sources
FSC® C104740

www.weidenfeldandnicolson.co.uk
www.orionbooks.co.uk

Praise for *The Secret Life of Writers*

'Wonderfully evocative . . . Musso's last novel, *The Reunion*, was breathtaking, but this is just as good. It casts a sinuous, sublime spell that lingers in the mind'   *Daily Mail*

Praise for *The Reunion*

'*The Reunion* will see him hailed as one of the great thriller writers of our age'   *Daily Express*

'Written with fluency and charm, this is breathtakingly good. Do not miss it'   *Daily Mail*

'Hugely enjoyable and beautifully staged, with an audacious authorial coup at the death that is simply breathtaking'
Irish Times

'Stylish and streamlined, nostalgic . . . More please'
The Times

'This immensely satisfying thriller had me turning the pages well into the night. *The Reunion* has everything a masterful thriller should: gut-wrenching suspense, a twisting story with blindsiding surprises, and a narrator with a mysterious past. It's no wonder that Guillaume Musso is one of France's most loved, bestselling authors'   Harlan Coben

'The perfect summer book to devour while lounging by a swimming pool'   *Elle*

Guillaume Musso is the no. 1 bestselling author in France. His novels have been translated into forty languages and sold over 33 million copies worldwide.

He was born in Antibes, in the south of France, and currently lives in Paris.

Vineet Lal studied French at the University of Edinburgh and Princeton University. He has translated several well-known French authors, including Michel Bussi and Grégoire Delacourt, and lives in Scotland.

For Nathan

To survive, you must tell stories.

Umberto Eco,
The Island of the Day Before

Saint-Julien-les-Roses

Landing stage

Convent of
Sainte-Sophie

Sainte-Sophie
peninsula

Colleen
Dunbar's
cottage

Tristana Beach

Mediterranean Sea

Le Safranier
Point

The Southern Cross

Silver Cove
Beach

Punta
dell'A

Pine Cove

Les Ondes Beach

Saragota Esplanade

Isle of Beaumont

N

W   E

S

PROLOGUE

THE NATHAN FAWLES MYSTERY

(*Le Soir*, 4 March 2017)

Nathan Fawles, author of the legendary *Lorelei Strange*, might have been absent from the literary scene for almost twenty years now, but he continues to hold a real fascination for readers of all ages. The writer, who currently lives in isolation on a Mediterranean island, has stubbornly turned down all requests for media interviews. *Le Soir* investigates the life of the Isle of Beaumont's shadowy recluse.

They call it the Streisand effect: the more you try hiding something, the more you make people curious about what you're trying to hide. Ever since his sudden exit from the literary world at the age of thirty-five, Fawles has been the victim of this perverse way of thinking. Shrouded in a veil of mystery, the life of this Franco-American author has generated more than its share of tittle-tattle and rumour throughout the last two decades.

Fawles was born in New York in 1964 to an American father and French mother, and spent his childhood near Paris before returning to the US to complete his education, first at Phillips Academy and then at Yale. After graduating in law and political science, he became involved in humanitarian causes, and spent a few years out in the field working for Action Against Hunger and Médecins Sans Frontières, notably in El Salvador, Armenia and Kurdistan.

THE SUCCESSFUL WRITER

He returned to New York in 1993 and published his first novel, *Loreleï Strange*, a rites-of-passage tale about an adolescent girl confined to a psychiatric hospital. This was no overnight hit, but in a matter of months, word of mouth – especially among teenage readers – catapulted the book to the top of the bestseller list. Two years later, with his second novel, *A Small American Town*, a vast ensemble piece of nearly a thousand pages, Fawles walked off with the Pulitzer Prize and established himself as one of the most original voices in American writing.

Towards the end of 1997, the author sprang his first surprise on the literary world. By then living in Paris, he chose to write his next book in French. *Les Foudroyés*, or *Thunderstruck*, was a heartrending love story – but also a meditation on grief, the human mind and the power of writing. This was really when French readers began to discover his work – not least because he also took part in a special edition of the literary talk show *Bouillon de culture*, along with Salman Rushdie, Umberto Eco and Mario Vargas Llosa. He featured in the programme once more in November 1998, for what would prove to be his penultimate media appearance. Indeed, seven months later, at barely thirty-five, he announced in a scathing interview with Agence France-Presse that he had made the irrevocable decision to give up writing.

A RECLUSE ON THE ISLE OF BEAUMONT

From then on, the author has clung resolutely to his position. Fawles – now well settled in his home on the Isle of Beaumont – hasn't published a single word ever since, nor granted a single interview to any journalist. He's also turned down all requests to adapt his novels for film or television (the latest to lose out being Netflix and Amazon, despite, allegedly, some very lucrative offers).

For almost twenty years now, the deafening silence of the 'Beaumont Recluse' has continued to fire the public imagination. Why would Nathan Fawles, at only thirty-five, and then at the height of his success, choose to retreat from the world of his own accord?

'There's no mystery surrounding Nathan Fawles,' says Jasper Van Wyck, his long-time agent. 'There's no big secret waiting to be revealed. Nathan's simply moved on to other things. He's drawn a line under his writing and the publishing world, once and for all.' Van Wyck remains vague when pressed on how the novelist now spends his time: 'As far as I know, Nathan's busy sorting out his personal affairs.'

A PRIVATE LIFE IS A PEACEFUL LIFE

To dampen reader expectations, his agent makes it clear that the author 'hasn't written a single line for twenty years.' He couldn't be more explicit: 'Even if *Lorelei Strange* has often been compared to *The Catcher in the Rye*, Fawles is no Salinger: there's no safe stuffed with manuscripts in his house. You won't see a new novel by Nathan Fawles ever again. Even after his death. That's a definite.'

A warning, however, that's never discouraged the curious from trying to find out more. Over the years, numerous readers and several journalists have trekked out to the Isle of Beaumont and prowled around Fawles's home. But they've always found the door firmly shut. This sense of distrust appears to have spread to the rest of the islanders too – hardly surprising in a place that, even before the writer's arrival, had established as its motto the maxim 'A private life is a peaceful life'.

The mayor's office limits itself to the briefest of statements: 'The local council is unable to comment on the identity of its residents, regardless of whether they are famous or not.' Locals willing to talk openly about the author of *Loreleï Strange* are thin on the ground. The few who did agree to be interviewed see the writer's presence on the island as nothing out of the ordinary. 'Oh, Nathan Fawles certainly doesn't spend his life locked away at home, or huddled up alone,' says Yvonne Sicard, the wife of Beaumont's only doctor. 'You'll often run into him driving his Mini Moke when he goes shopping at Ed's Corner – that's our local store, the only one in town.'

He's also frequently seen at the island's pub, 'especially when there's a match with Olympique de Marseille on TV,' says the owner. According to one of the regulars, 'Nathan simply isn't the barbarian they talk about in the papers. In fact, he's an incredibly nice guy – he really knows his football, and he loves Japanese whisky.' There's just one topic of conversation that's likely to get him worked up: 'If you try getting him onto his books, or literature, he'll end up walking out.'

A VOID IN LITERATURE

When it comes to his fellow writers, you'll find Nathan Fawles has a great many fans. Tom Boyd, for example, is one of those devoted followers who can't praise him enough. 'I've read a great many authors, but his books always leave me incredibly moved. There's no doubt he's right up there, among the writers to whom I'll for ever be in debt,' says the creator of *The Angel Trilogy*. A view echoed by Thomas Degalais, who feels that Fawles – in the course of three very different books – has created a highly original body of work which will inevitably leave its mark: 'Naturally, I'm sorry he's left the literary stage – we all feel that way,' says the French novelist. 'We're living through times that cry out for his voice. I'd love Nathan to write a new book and step back into the spotlight, but I'm afraid that's never going to happen.'

Which indeed seems very likely – but let's not forget that Fawles chose these words from *King Lear* as the epigraph to his last novel:

> It is the stars,
> The stars above us, govern our conditions

Jean-Michel Dubois

THE WRITER WHO'D GIVEN UP WRITING

Éditions Calmann-Lévy
21 Rue du Montparnasse
75006 Paris

Our ref: 379529

> M. Raphaël Bataille
> 75 Avenue Aristide Briand
> 92120 Montrouge

> Paris, 28 May 2018

Monsieur,

Thank you for sending us your manuscript of *Crown Shyness*, and for your keen interest in Éditions Calmann-Lévy.

Our reading committee has considered your submission very carefully, but regretfully it doesn't quite match the profile of new titles we are currently seeking for our list.

We wish you every success in finding a publisher for your book very soon.

Kind regards,

> Editorial Department

PS: Your manuscript is available for you to collect from our office for the next month. If you would prefer to have it returned by post, please send us a self-addressed envelope with the correct postage.

1

THE ESSENTIAL QUALITY
IN A WRITER

Tuesday, 11 September 2018

1.

The wind was slapping at the sails in a dazzling sky.

The dinghy had left the Var coast a little after 1 p.m., and was now flying along at a speed of five knots towards the Isle of Beaumont. Sitting near the helm, just beside the skipper, I was bewitched by the spell of the breeze from the sea, completely transfixed as I gazed at the dusting of gold that glittered across the Mediterranean.

That very morning, I had left my studio near Paris to catch the 6 a.m. high-speed train bound for Avignon. From the historic city of the Popes, I had taken a bus to Hyères, and then a taxi to the tiny port of Saint-Julien-les-Roses, sole departure point for ferries over to the Isle of Beaumont. Because of yet another delay – the umpteenth – on the French railways, I had missed the one and only lunchtime shuttle by five minutes. While I was roaming around the quay, dragging my case behind me, the captain of a Dutch sailing boat who was getting ready to fetch his passengers from the island had kindly offered to take me with him.

So here I was, a young man who'd just turned twenty-four, at a tricky time in my life. Two years earlier, I had graduated from a business school in Paris, but I hadn't bothered looking for a job to match my skills and experience. I'd really only done this degree to reassure my parents, and I didn't care much for a future played out to the tune of management, marketing and money. Over the last two years, I had juggled the odd job here and there to pay my rent, but I had devoted all of my creative energy to writing a novel, *Crown Shyness*, which had just been turned down by a dozen publishers. I had pinned each of my rejection letters to the noticeboard above my desk, and so profound was my sense of despair – matched only by my passion for writing – that every time I drove a pin into the cork, it felt as though I were plunging it straight into my heart.

Thankfully, I never remained depressed for very long. Until now, I had always managed to convince myself that these failures were merely the precursor to success. To bolster this belief, I clung on to some illustrious examples. Stephen King often talked about how thirty publishers had turned down *Carrie*. Half the publishers in London had found the first Harry Potter book 'far too long for children'. Before becoming the world's bestselling science fiction novel, Frank Herbert's *Dune* had been knocked back around twenty times. And as for F. Scott Fitzgerald, he had – apparently – papered the walls of his office with the one hundred and twenty-two rejection letters sent by the magazines to which he'd offered his short stories.

2.

But the cracks were beginning to show in this strategy of positive thinking. Despite mustering all of my willpower, I had difficulty getting back into writing. It wasn't blank page syndrome or a lack of ideas that left me paralysed. It was the pernicious impression of not making any progress in my chosen field. The feeling of not knowing exactly what direction to take. I could have done with a fresh pair of eyes on my work. Someone who was benevolent yet uncompromising. At the start of the year, I had signed up to a creative writing course organised by a prestigious publishing house. I had pinned all my hopes on this workshop, but I was quickly disillusioned. The writer leading it – Bernard Dufy, a novelist who'd seen his finest hour during the 1990s – presented himself as a *stylesmith*, to borrow his own expression. 'All of your work has to focus on *language* and not the story,' he kept saying the entire time. 'The narrative exists purely to serve *language*. A book should have no other aim but the quest for form, rhythm and harmony. Language is the one place you can still be original – because, ever since Shakespeare, there's been no more stories left to write.'

The 1000 euros I'd forked out on this writing course – for three sessions, each of four hours – had left me furious, and penniless into the bargain. Perhaps Dufy was right, but personally I thought precisely the opposite: style wasn't an end in itself. The essential quality in a writer was knowing how to captivate their reader through a good story. A narrative that was capable of wrenching them out of their own existence, and thrusting them deep into the intimacy and reality of its characters. Style was simply a means of connecting a nerve supply to the narrative and bringing it to life. Deep down, I didn't care about the opinion of an academic writer like Dufy. The only opinion I'd have liked to have, and the only one that would have been important, in my view, belonged to someone I had always idolised: Nathan Fawles, my favourite author.

I had discovered his books towards the end of my adolescence, by which point Fawles hadn't written a thing for a long time. *Les Foudroyés*, his third novel, had been given to me by Diane Laborie, my girlfriend in my final year at school, by way of a breaking-up present. The novel had shaken me more than the death of a romance that had never really been one at all. I had moved on seamlessly to his first two books: *Loreleï Strange* and *A Small American Town*. I would never read anything quite as inspiring ever again.

Through his unique writing, Fawles seemed to be speaking directly to me. His novels were fluid, vibrant and intense. I've never been a great fan of any particular author, and yet I had read and reread his books because they talked about me, about connecting with others, the challenge of steering the ship of life, the vulnerability of men and the fragility of our existence. They gave me strength and heightened my desire to write.

In the years following his literary exit, other authors had tried slipping into his style, absorbing the essence of his world, imitating his way of constructing a narrative or mimicking his sensitivity. But for me, no one had managed to come anywhere close. There was only one Nathan Fawles. Whether you liked him or not, you were forced to admit that Fawles was an exceptional novelist. Even if you didn't know it was his work, it was enough to skim a single page from one of his books to know he was the one who'd written it. And I've always considered this to be the true mark of talent.

I, too, had dissected his novels to try to unlock their secrets, and harboured the ambition of making contact with him. Despite being pessimistic about my chances of getting an answer, I'd written to him several times via his French publisher and his agent in the US. I had also sent him my manuscript.

Then, ten days earlier, I'd spotted a job offer in the newsletter sent out by the Isle of Beaumont's official website. The Scarlet Rose, the island's little bookshop, was looking to take on some help. I'd applied right away by sending an email to the bookseller and, the very same day, Grégoire Audibert, the shop's owner, had called me via FaceTime to let me know I'd been successful. He needed someone for three months. The salary was no great shakes, but he was willing to guarantee my accommodation and two meals a day at The Taming of the Stew, one of the restaurants on the square in Beaumont's only town.

I was delighted to have landed a job that – from what I was led to believe by Audibert – would leave me time to write in an inspirational setting. And which, I was convinced, would give me the opportunity to meet Nathan Fawles.

3.

The skipper carried out a deft manoeuvre and slowed the boat down.

'Land ahoy!' he shouted, cocking his chin at the island silhouetted on the horizon.

Situated three-quarters of an hour by boat from the Var coast, the Isle of Beaumont was shaped like a crescent. An arc which was approximately fifteen kilometres long by six wide. It was always portrayed as a wild, unspoilt setting. One of the pearls of the Mediterranean, where creeks bubbling with turquoise water, rocky inlets, pine forests and pristine sandy beaches alternated with each other. An eternal Côte d'Azur, without tourists, pollution or concrete.

During the previous ten days, I'd had plenty of time to pore over all the information I'd managed to dig up regarding the island. Since 1955, Beaumont had belonged to a reclusive family of Italian industrialists, the Gallinaris, who, at the beginning of the 1960s, had invested ludicrous sums of money in major improvements, spearheading large-scale projects to supply water and level the earth, and creating one of the first marinas on the coast from scratch. As the years passed, development on the island had continued in line with one cardinal principle: never to sacrifice the well-being of its inhabitants on the altar of so-called modernity. And for the islanders, this threat was personified in two easily recognised ways: property speculators and tourists.

To limit new construction, the local council had adopted a simple rule that consisted of capping the overall number of water meters. A strategy that copied what the little town of Bolinas in California had been doing for a long time. The result being that, for thirty years, the population had hovered around the one thousand five hundred mark. There were no estate agents on Beaumont: a certain percentage of property would be passed on from one family to another, and the rest sold through personal connections. As for tourism, this was kept in check by carefully controlling transport links with the mainland. Whether in high season or the depths of winter, just a single shuttle – the celebrated *Audacious*, which locals somewhat grandly referred to as 'the ferry' – made three return journeys a day (and no more) at 8 a.m., 12.30 p.m. and 7 p.m., from the harbour on Beaumont to the quayside at Saint-Julien-les-Roses. All of this was done the old-fashioned way: you couldn't book in advance, and priority was always given to the islanders.

To be precise, Beaumont wasn't hostile to the arrival of tourists, but no real provision had been made for them. All in all, the island had three cafés, two restaurants and one pub. There were no hotels and accommodation in private homes was rare. Yet the more you dissuaded people from coming, the more mysterious the place became, and the greater its appeal. Alongside the local population, there were also some wealthy individuals who owned holiday homes on the island. Over the decades, industrialists and a few artistic types had raved about this idyllic setting, so chic and yet so relaxing too. The owner of a high-tech company and two or three leading figures in the wine industry had managed to acquire some villas. But no matter how famous or wealthy, everyone kept a low profile. The community wasn't resistant to assimilating new members, on condition they accepted the values that had governed the soul of Beaumont since time began. In any case, the recent arrivals often proved to be the fiercest at defending their adopted island home.

This social exclusivity provoked a great deal of criticism – indeed, it infuriated those who were left out. At the start of the 1980s, the socialist government had nurtured vague hopes of repurchasing Beaumont – allegedly to designate it as a protected site, but in reality to put an end to the island's special status. A general outcry had ensued and the government had been forced to back down. Since that time, the civil service had come to terms with things: the Isle of Beaumont was a distinctive place in its own right. And it really did exist, just a stone's throw from the Var coast. A little paradise lapped by crystal-clear waters. A tiny bit of France that wasn't really France at all.

4.

Once back on land, I dragged my case along the cobbles on the quayside. The marina wasn't very big, but it was well developed, a lively harbour full of charm. The little town was spread out around the bay, a bit like an amphitheatre: tiers of colourful houses which glinted under a metallic sky. Their bright hues and the way they were laid out reminded me of the Greek island of Hydra, which I'd visited as a teenager with my parents; but a moment later, as I wandered through narrow, sloping alleys, I found myself in the Italy of the 1960s. Later still, having climbed higher up, I caught my first glimpse of the beaches with their white dunes, and I thought of the vast, sandy shores of Massachusetts. During this first encounter with the island, as my case rattled along the cobbled streets leading to the centre of the town, I realised that the distinctiveness and magic of Beaumont stemmed precisely from this indefinable mishmash. Beaumont was a chameleon of a place: somewhere unique and unclassifiable, which it was pointless ever hoping to analyse or explain.

I soon arrived on the main square. Given its resemblance to a Provençal village, it suddenly felt as though the town had sprung from a novel by Jean Giono. The Place des Martyrs was the beating heart of Beaumont. A shady esplanade, surrounded by a clock tower, a war memorial, a babbling fountain and an area devoted to playing boules. Under vine-covered pergolas, nestling amicably against each other, sat the island's two restaurants: Wuthering Bites and The Taming of the Stew. I recognised the lean physique of Grégoire Audibert sitting outside the latter, where he was polishing off some artichokes à la poivrade. He resembled an old-fashioned schoolteacher: salt-and-pepper beard, short waistcoat and a long jacket in crushed linen.

The bookseller recognised me too and, like a true gentleman, invited me over to his table. He offered me a lemonade as if I were twelve years old.

'I'd best tell you straight away: I'm shutting the shop at the end of the year,' he announced bluntly.

'How come?'

'That's why I'm looking to take someone on: to do some tidying up, a bit of bookkeeping and one big final stocktake.'

'So you're closing down for good?'

He nodded, mopping up the last drops of olive oil with his bread.

'What for?'

'I can't take any more of this. Business has been going down steadily for years, and it's not going to get any better. Anyhow, you know the score yourself: the authorities let the online giants thrive in peace and quiet, and those guys don't even pay taxes in France.'

Audibert sighed, remained pensive for a few seconds and then added, half fatalistic, half provocative:

'And let's be realistic too: why bother going to a shop when you can have a book delivered in three clicks on your iPhone?'

'For loads of reasons! Have you tried finding a buyer?'

The bookseller shrugged.

'No one's interested. There's nothing less profitable these days than books. My shop's not the first to close, and it certainly won't be the last.'

He emptied the rest of his carafe of wine into his glass and drank it in one go.

'Come, I'll show you round The Scarlet Rose,' he said, folding his napkin and rising to his feet.

Trailing behind him, I crossed the square to the bookshop. The window, which was horrendously dull, displayed books that had probably been gathering dust for months. Audibert pushed the door open and stepped aside to let me past.

The shop's interior was just as dreary. Curtains robbed the place of any light. The walnut shelves certainly had character, yet they housed nothing but the most classical of the classics: an indigestible, frankly snobbish selection of titles.

Culture at its most academic. I was only just beginning to figure Audibert out, but – from what I'd seen so far – I fleetingly imagined him having a heart attack were he obliged to sell science-fiction, fantasy or mangas.

'I'll let you see your room,' he said, pointing to a wooden staircase at the back of the shop.

Audibert's apartment was on the first floor. My accommodation was located on the second: a long, narrow studio under the eaves. As I opened the creaking French windows, I was pleasantly surprised to discover a balcony with a terrace overlooking the square. The spectacular view which stretched as far as the sea lifted my spirits a little. A maze of alleys snaked between the ochre buildings with their weathered stone before reaching the shore.

After putting my things away, I came down to meet Audibert in the shop to run through precisely what he expected of me.

'The Wi-Fi doesn't work very well,' he warned as he switched on an old PC. 'You often need to restart the router – you'll find it upstairs.'

Leaving the computer to wake up, Audibert plugged in a small electric hob and filled the base of an Italian espresso pot.

'Coffee?'

'Yes, please.'

While he was making our coffee, I wandered into the shop. Pinned to the large cork noticeboard behind the desk were some old front covers of the publishing weekly *Livres Hebdo*, dating back to the time when Romain Gary was still writing (and that's hardly an exaggeration). I felt like throwing the curtains wide open, whipping away the threadbare purple rugs and reorganising every square inch of the shelves and display tables.

As if he'd been reading my mind, Audibert shared his thoughts.

'The Scarlet Rose has been around since 1967. The bookshop isn't much to look at now, but at one time it was quite an institution. A great many authors, both French and from overseas, would come here to meet the public and sign books.'

He pulled a leather-bound visitors' book from a drawer and held it out, encouraging me to leaf through it. And indeed, as the photos flicked by, one after the other, I recognised Michel Tournier, J.M.G. Le Clézio, Françoise Sagan, Jean d'Ormesson, John Irving, John le Carré and . . . Nathan Fawles.

'Are you really going to close?'

'I don't feel bad about it,' he said. 'People don't read nowadays. That's just how it is.'

I qualified his statement:

'Maybe people are reading in a different way, but they're still reading.'

He turned down the hob to stop the coffee pot from whistling.

'Anyway, you know what I mean. I'm not talking about frothier stuff, I'm talking *real* literature.'

Ah yes, the much-vaunted 'real literature' . . .

There was always a moment with people like Audibert when this expression – or another one, 'real writer' – came up for debate yet again. Well, I had never let anyone tell me what I ought to read or not. And setting yourself up as a judge like this to decide what was or wasn't literature felt like pretension of the highest possible order.

'Do you know many real readers among the people around you?' asked the bookseller, beginning to get heated. 'I'm talking intelligent readers. The ones who spend significant time reading serious books.'

Without waiting for me to reply, he carried on, his anger rising:

'Between you and me, how many real readers are there left in France? Ten thousand? Five thousand? Even fewer, perhaps.'

'I think you're being pessimistic.'

'No, no! You need to face facts: we're heading into a literary desert. Nowadays everyone wants to be a writer and no one's actually doing any reading.'

Searching for a way out of this conversation, I showed him the photo of Fawles stuck into the album.

'So, Nathan Fawles – do you know him?'

Audibert frowned. He had a wary look on his face.

'A bit. That is, assuming anyone could ever know Nathan Fawles . . .'

He handed me a cup of coffee which had the colour and consistency of ink.

'When Fawles came here to sign his books in 1995, or 1996, it was the first time he'd ever set foot on the island. He fell in love with it at once. In fact, I was the one who helped him buy his house, The Southern Cross. But since then we've had virtually no contact at all.'

'Does he still come to the bookshop, now and then?'

'No, never.'

'If I went to see him, do you think he'd agree to sign a book for me?'

Audibert shook his head and sighed.

'I'd strongly suggest you forget that idea. It's the best way of getting yourself shot.'

AGENCE FRANCE-PRESSE INTERVIEW WITH NATHAN FAWLES

AFP – 12 June 1999 (extract)

Can you confirm that at thirty-five, at the height of your fame, you're calling time on your career as a novelist?

Yes, I'm done with all that. I've been a serious writer for ten years now. Ten years of plonking my ass on a chair every morning, with my eyes glued to my keyboard. I don't want to live like that ever again.

Is that your final decision?

Yes. Art is long. And life is short.

Last year, however, you announced you were working on a new novel, provisionally called *An Invincible Summer* . . .

The project didn't make it any further than a rough outline. I've abandoned it, once and for all.

What message would you like to send to the many readers who're waiting for your next book?

There's no point waiting. I'm not writing any more books.

They should read other authors. There's no shortage of those.

Is writing difficult?
Yes, but probably less so than many other jobs. What's complicated and nerve-wracking is the irrational side of writing: the fact you've written three novels doesn't mean you know how to write the fourth. There's no method, or rules, or road map. Every time you begin a new novel, it's the same leap into the unknown.

So, are you good at anything apart from writing?
Apparently I make a really mean blanquette de veau.

Do you think your novels will stand the test of time?
I sincerely hope not.

What role can literature play in contemporary society?
I've never asked myself that question and I've no intention of starting now.

You've also decided not to give any more interviews?
I've already done too many . . . It's a cosmetic exercise that doesn't mean anything now, except to create some buzz. Most of the time, if not always, they report your words inaccurately, or chop them up, or take them out of context. I've tried my best, but I can't get any satisfaction from 'explaining' my novels. And even less from answering questions about my political leanings, or my private life.

Yet surely knowing more about the life of writers you admire allows you to understand their work better . . .

Like Margaret Atwood, or rather that little saying she quotes, I think wanting to meet an author because you like their books is like wanting to meet a duck because you like pâté.

But isn't it legitimate to want to question a writer about the meaning of their work?

No, it's not legitimate at all. The only valid relationship with a writer is reading what they've written.

2

LEARNING TO WRITE

A week later

Tuesday, 18 September 2018

1.

With my head down, and my hands clenched on the handle-bars, I gave one last push on the pedals to reach the summit of the northern tip of the island. I was dripping with sweat. My rented bike felt as if it weighed a ton, and my backpack was digging into my shoulders.

It hadn't taken me long to fall in love with Beaumont too. During the week I'd been living here, I'd made the most of my free time to explore every corner of the island and get to know its topography.

By now, I practically knew the north coast of Beaumont by heart. This was where the harbour, the only town and the most attractive beaches were to be found. Dominated by cliffs and rocks, the west coast was less accessible, and wilder, but no less beautiful. I had only ventured out there once, onto the Sainte-Sophie peninsula, to catch a glimpse of the convent of the same name where twenty or so Benedictine nuns still lived.

At the other end, Le Safranier Point, where I was heading now, wasn't connected via the Strada Principale, the forty-odd-kilometre road that went right around the island. To get there, you had to go beyond the last of the northern beaches – Silver Cove – and follow a narrow dirt track for two kilometres through the middle of a pine forest.

Based on the information I'd managed to glean during the week, the entrance to Nathan Fawles's property was located at the end of this trail, which answered to the pretty name of Botanists' Path. When I finally got there, all I found was an aluminium gate set in a tall rubble-stone wall, made of schist, which surrounded the estate. No letterbox, nor any mention of the owner. The house was theoretically called The Southern Cross, but this wasn't marked anywhere. Only a handful of signs extended the warmest of welcomes: 'Private Property', 'No Entry', 'Beware of the Dog', 'Property under Video Surveillance' . . . There wasn't even the possibility of ringing a bell, or signalling one's presence in any way at all. The message was abundantly clear: 'Whoever you are, you're not welcome.'

I dumped my bike and walked along the outer wall. At a certain point, the forest gave way to scrubland, dense with heather, myrtle and wild lavender. After five hundred metres, I emerged onto a cliff that plunged into the sea.

At the risk of breaking a few bones, I slid down the rocks until I found a secure foothold. I scrambled along the sheer side of the precipice and managed to clamber back over the edge at a spot where the rock face was less steep. Having cleared this obstacle, I carried on along the coast for about fifty metres and then, as I rounded a massive stony outcrop, it finally sprang into view: the home of Nathan Fawles.

The villa was built into the side of a cliff and seemed to be embedded within the living rock. In the great tradition of modern architecture, it was a rectangular cuboid, ribbed with slabs of unfinished reinforced concrete. Three distinct levels stood out, flanked by terraces and served by a stone staircase leading directly to the sea. The base of the building appeared to merge into the cliff itself. It was punctured by a series of portholes, like an ocean liner, and by a tall, wide shutter that suggested it was used as a boathouse. In front of it jutted a wooden pontoon, at the end of which was moored a speedboat with a glistening wooden hull.

As I continued making careful progress over the rocks, I thought I could see a shadow moving around on the middle terrace. Could this possibly be Fawles himself? I shaded my eyes with my hand, trying to make out the figure more clearly. It was a man. A man who, at that precise moment, was . . . aiming at me with a shotgun.

2.

I barely had time to fling myself behind a rock when a shot rang through the air. Four or five metres behind me, the bullet exploded in a shower of shrapnel which crackled in my ears. I was paralysed with fear for a good minute or so. My heart was pounding. My whole body was shaking and a trickle of sweat ran down my back. Audibert hadn't been lying. Fawles had completely lost the plot, and was using anyone who trespassed on his property as a target for clay pigeon shooting. I remained pinned to the ground. I had stopped breathing. Having had this initial warning, my brain was screaming at me to run for my life straight away. But I decided not to pull back. On the contrary, I picked myself up again and kept advancing towards the house. By now, Fawles had come down to the lowest level, to a raised area of paving overlooking the rocks. A second shot hit a tree trunk that the wind must have brought down. The log shattered, spraying fragments of dead wood which grazed my face. I was more scared than I'd ever been in my life. Yet, almost despite myself, I stubbornly carried on, leaping from one rock to another. Nathan Fawles, the man whose novels I had loved so much, couldn't possibly be a killer in the making. As if to underline how very wrong I was, a third shot sent the dust flying a mere fifty centimetres from my Converse trainers.

Soon, I was only a few metres away from him.

'Get the hell out! You're on private property!' he shouted down from the paved terrace.

'That's no reason to shoot at me!'

'It is, for me!'

I had the sun in my eyes. Fawles stood framed against the light, his silhouette nearly impossible to make out. He was of average height, but solidly built, wearing a Panama hat and sunglasses with a bluish tint. Crucially, he still had his gun pointed at me, ready to fire.

'What the fuck are you doing here?'

'I've come to see you, Monsieur Fawles.'

I slipped off my backpack to take out the manuscript of *Crown Shyness*.

'My name's Raphaël Bataille. I've written a novel. I'd like you to read it and tell me what you think.'

'I don't give a shit about your novel. And nothing gives you the right to come and harass me at home.'

'I respect you too much to harass you.'

'But that's just what you're doing. If you really respected me, you'd also respect my right not to be disturbed.'

A magnificent dog – a fair-haired golden retriever – had just bounded up to Fawles on the terrace and was barking at me.

'Why the heck did you keep going? I was still shooting!'

'I knew you wouldn't kill me.'

'Why not?'

'Because you wrote *Loreleï Strange* and *Les Foudroyés*.'

Still blinded by the light in my eyes, I heard him snigger.

'If you think writers have the same moral virtues they give their characters, then you're really naive. And even a bit thick.'

'Listen, I'd just like some advice from you. To improve my writing.'

'Advice? Believe me, kid, no writer's ever got better through advice! If you had even a drop of common sense, you'd have figured that out already by yourself.'

'Giving some thought to others never hurt anyone.'

'No one can *teach* you to write. It's something you have to learn on your own.'

Fawles looked thoughtful, and lowered his guard for a second to stroke his dog's head before going on:

'OK, you wanted some advice, and you've got it. Piss off now.'

'Can I leave you my manuscript?' I asked, pulling the bound pages from my backpack.

'Nope, I'm not reading it. No way.'

'Jeez, you're awkward.'

'But I'll chuck in some more advice for free: do something else with your life, apart from wanting to be a writer.'

'That's what my parents say all the time.'

'Well, that proves they're not half as thick as you.'

3.

There was a sudden gust of wind, and a wave came sweeping up to the rocky spur where I was perched. I scrambled up another cluster of boulders to escape, which brought me even closer to the writer. He had his pump-action shotgun pressed tight against his shoulder again. A Remington Wingmaster with dual action bars – the kind you sometimes saw in old movies, even though this one was shaped more like a hunting rifle.

'What was your name again?' he asked when the water had ebbed away.

'Raphaël, Raphaël Bataille.'

'And how old are you?'

'Twenty-four.'

'How long have you wanted to write?'

'Always. That's all I've ever wanted.'

Making the most of the fact that I had his attention, I launched into a monologue to explain just how important reading and writing had been for me, ever since childhood, how they'd been my lifelines, helping me endure the mediocrity and absurdity of the world. How much strength I'd gained, thanks to books, building myself an internal fortress which . . .

'You gonna reel off your clichés for a while?' he interrupted.

'They're not clichés,' I protested, feeling rather hurt as I put my manuscript away in the backpack.

'If I were your age now, I'd have other ambitions than wanting to become a writer.'

'Why?'

'Because being a writer is the least glamorous thing in the world,' sighed Fawles. 'You live like a zombie, all alone and cut off from everyone else. You spend all day in your pyjamas ruining your eyes in front of a screen, stuffing your face with cold pizza and talking to imaginary characters who end up driving you nuts. You spend your nights sweating blood and tears to churn out a sentence that three-quarters of your readers won't even notice – the handful of readers you have, that is. That's what it's like, being a writer.'

'Um, there's more to it than that—'

Fawles continued as if he hadn't heard a thing.

'And worst of all, you end up getting hooked on this shitty existence because you give yourself the illusion, what with your pen and your keyboard, that you're some kind of god and can patch up the holes in real life.'

'Easy for you to say that. You've had it all.'

'What have I had?'

'Millions of readers, fame, money, literary prizes. All those women you've slept with.'

'Frankly, if you're writing for money or women, I'd do something else.'

'You see what I mean.'

'No. And I don't even know why I'm talking to you.'

'I'm leaving you my manuscript.'

Fawles began to protest, but as fast as I could I hurled the backpack at the terrace where he was standing.

Startled, the writer tried to get out of the way to avoid being hit. His right foot slipped and he fell onto the rock.

He stifled a cry and tried to get up again immediately, letting out an expletive:

'What the fuck! My ankle!'

'Oh God, I'm so sorry. Hang on, I'm coming to help.'

'Don't move! If you want to help, get the hell out of here. And don't you ever come back.'

He picked up his weapon and took aim. This time I was utterly convinced he was capable of gunning me down on the spot. I whirled around and fled, slipping and sliding over the rocks, catching myself from falling – first with one hand, then the other – in the most undignified manner to escape the writer's fury.

As I was scrambling away, I wondered why Nathan Fawles now had such a jaded view of life. I had read a number of interviews he'd given prior to 1999. Before exiting the literary scene, Fawles hadn't needed persuading to engage with the media. He would always trot out a few kind words, and highlight his love for reading and writing. What could possibly have tipped him over the edge?

Why would a man at the peak of his fame suddenly abandon everything he loves doing, everything that makes him who he is, that nourishes him, only to lock himself away in isolation? What had gone so horribly wrong in Fawles's life, to such an extent that he'd give it all up? A deep depression? A bereavement? An illness? No one had ever been able to answer those questions. Something told me that, if I managed to solve the Nathan Fawles mystery, I would also succeed in making my dream of publishing a book come true.

Back in the forest, I leapt on my bike and made for the road leading back to the town. My day had been productive. Fawles might not have given me the writing lesson I was expecting, but he'd gone one better: he'd given me a terrific subject for a novel and the energy I needed to start writing it.

3

WRITERS AND THEIR
SHOPPING LISTS

Three weeks later

Monday, 8 October 2018

1.

Nathan Fawles was worried sick.

He was partly stretched out in an armchair, with his right foot, in plaster, resting on a fluffy ottoman. He felt utterly distraught. His dog Bronco – the sole being whose existence on earth mattered to him – had been missing for two days. The golden retriever would occasionally disappear for an hour or two, but never more. There was no doubt whatsoever: something had happened to him. He'd been in an accident, or injured. Or stolen.

The previous evening, Nathan had called his agent to seek his advice. Jasper Van Wyck, a New Yorker, was his principal link to the world and the closest thing he had to a friend. Jasper had volunteered to ring round all the local shops and businesses on Beaumont. He'd also had a small poster put together by one of the members of his team, offering a reward of 1000 euros to whoever found the dog, and had sent it to each of the island's traders by email. Now there was nothing left to do but wait, and hope for the best.

Nathan sighed, staring at his plastered ankle. He already felt like having a whisky, despite the fact that it wasn't even 11 a.m. Twenty days of being cooped up inside, all because of that little dickhead Raphaël Bataille. To begin with, he'd thought the sprain was just a minor one, and he'd get away with an ice pack on the joint and a few paracetamols. But waking up the day after the kid's rude intrusion, he'd realised things were going to be a lot more complicated. Not only had the swelling on his ankle not gone down, but he'd also found it impossible to take a single step without screaming in agony.

He'd finally had to resign himself to calling Jean-Louis Sicard, the sole doctor on Beaumont. Sicard was a bit of a character, who'd spent thirty years roaming all over the island on an old moped. His diagnosis hadn't sounded good. The ankle ligaments had torn, the joint capsule had ripped open and one of the tendons had suffered badly too.

The doctor had prescribed complete rest. And, more importantly, he'd encased his foot in a plaster cast that almost went up to his knee, and which had been driving Fawles insane for three weeks.

The writer paced up and down on his crutches like a caged lion, guzzling anticoagulants to prevent his blood clotting. Thankfully, in less than twenty-four hours the bells of liberation would ring, loud and clear. He hardly ever used his phone, but that morning, at the crack of dawn, he'd reluctantly put in a call to Sicard to check he'd not forgotten their appointment. Fawles had even tried to persuade the old doctor to come round the same day, but his attempt had ended in failure.

2.

The ringing of the phone on the wall yanked Fawles out of his lethargy. The writer had neither a mobile nor a computer, nor an email address. Just an old Bakelite telephone attached to a load-bearing wooden pillar which demarcated the boundary between the living room and the kitchen. Fawles only used this device to make calls; he never answered the phone himself, preferring to let the answering machine upstairs kick in automatically. Today, however, his dog's disappearance had forced him to break with his habits. He stood up and, leaning on his crutches, dragged himself over to the phone.

It was Jasper Van Wyck.

'Great news, Nathan! They've found Bronco!'

Fawles was overcome by a huge sense of relief.

'Is he OK?'

'He's just fine,' his agent assured him.

'Where did they find him?'

'A young woman spotted him on the road, over towards the Sainte-Sophie peninsula, and took him to Ed's Corner.'

'Did you tell Ed to bring Bronco back?'

'This girl insists on doing it herself.'

Nathan smelt a rat. The peninsula was at the other end

43

of Beaumont, on completely the opposite side from Le Safranier Point. What if this woman had abducted his dog purely as a means of contacting him? In the early 1980s, a journalist, Betty Eppes, had deceived J.D. Salinger by lying about her identity and turning a trite conversation she'd had with him into an interview which she'd offered to the US press.

'So who exactly is she, this woman?'

'Mathilde Monney. Swiss, I believe, on vacation on the island. She's staying at the bed and breakfast near the Benedictine convent. She's a journalist with *Le Temps*, in Geneva.'

Fawles sighed. Why couldn't she have been a florist, or owned a deli, or been a nurse, or an airline pilot . . . Nope, she had to be a *journalist*.

'Forget it, Jasper. It all sounds a bit fishy.'

He clenched his fist and punched the wooden pillar. He needed his dog, and Bronco needed him. If only he'd been able to go and pick him up in his car. Yet that was no reason to fall into a trap. A journalist with *Le Temps* . . . He recalled a reporter from the same paper who'd once interviewed him in New York. A guy who'd colluded with him on a flattering piece, but who'd completely missed the point of the novel. Those were possibly the worst of all: journalists who wrote a good review of your book without having understood a single thing.

'Perhaps it's simply a coincidence she's a journalist?' suggested Jasper.

'A coincidence? You just being dumb, or taking the piss?'

'Listen, don't let it get to you, Nathan. You let her come to The Southern Cross, you get your dog back and then you chuck her out, pronto.'

Fawles rubbed his eyes to give himself a few more seconds to think. He felt vulnerable with his ankle in plaster, and hated this feeling of being thrown unwillingly into a situation over which he had no control.

'Fine,' he said, relenting despite his unease. 'Call her back, call this Mathilde Monney. Tell her to drop by in the early afternoon and give her directions for getting here.'

3.

Midday. After twenty minutes of persuasive reasoning, I'd just managed to sell a copy of the manga *A Distant Neighbourhood*, Taniguchi's masterpiece. I smiled to myself. In less than a month, I'd succeeded in transforming the shop. It wasn't so much a metamorphosis as a series of significant changes: a space that was now brighter and airier, and a welcome that felt warmer and less surly. I had even twisted Audibert's arm into letting me order a few books that were more about encouraging escapism than deep introspection. Little signals which all pointed in the same direction: culture was something that could also be *enjoyed*.

I had to give the bookseller due credit for giving me a free hand. He left me to my own devices and wasn't in the shop very often, only leaving his first-floor apartment when he went for a drink on the square. When I delved into the accounts, I realised he'd painted a far bleaker picture of things than they really merited. The shop's financial position was nowhere near as precarious as he'd made out. The premises belonged to Audibert and, like several traders on Beaumont, he received a generous subsidy from SA Gallinari, the company that owned the island. With a can-do attitude and plenty of energy, it was entirely feasible to restore the bookshop to its former glory, and even – this was my dream – attract authors back.

'Raphaël?'

Peter McFarlane, the owner of the bakery on the square, had just popped his head round the door. He was a good-natured Scotsman who, twenty-five years earlier, had left one island for another. His shop was renowned for its southern French specialities – savoury pissaladière and sweet fougassette. It rejoiced in the name of Bread Pit, thereby respecting a tradition that was faintly absurd, and utterly at odds with Beaumont's chic aura, but to which the locals seemed very attached: giving each business a name based on a play on words. Only the odd spoilsport like Ed had refused to play along.

'You up for an aperitif?' asked Peter.

Every day, someone would invite me to partake in the ritual of pre-lunch drinks. At the stroke of midday, people would seat themselves on café terraces to enjoy a pastis or a glass of Terra dei Pini, the white wine that was the island's pride and joy. At first, it had all felt a bit quaint, but I quickly found myself going with the flow. Everyone knew everyone on Beaumont. Wherever you went, you would always run into a familiar face and have a little chat. People took time to live life and talk to each other, and for someone like myself who had always lived surrounded by the drabness, pollution and aggressive behaviour of the Paris region, this was something of a novelty.

I sat down with Peter on the terrace at Yeast of Eden. I scanned the faces around me, feigning an air of indifference as I looked for a young blonde woman. One of the customers from the shop whom I'd happened to meet the previous day. Her name was Mathilde Monney. She was on holiday on Beaumont where she had taken a room in a house near the Benedictine convent. She'd bought all three novels by Nathan Fawles, assuring me, however, that she'd read them already. Bright, witty, dazzling. We had chatted for twenty minutes and I still hadn't got over it. I'd been obsessed with the thought of seeing her again ever since.

The only damper on these recent weeks was that I hadn't written very much. My project on the Nathan Fawles mystery – which I'd christened *The Secret Life of Writers* – had scarcely made any progress. I had very little to work on and my subject was proving elusive. I'd sent several emails to Jasper Van Wyck, Fawles's agent, who of course hadn't replied; I'd interviewed various people on the island, but no one had told me anything I didn't know already.

'So, what's this story about some nutter?' asked Audibert as he joined us, a glass of rosé in his hand.

The bookseller looked worried. A bizarre rumour had been sweeping across the square for ten minutes, and now more and more people were converging there. It concerned the discovery of a body by two Dutch hikers on Tristana Beach, the only beach on the south-west coast of the island. A stunning location, but a dangerous one too. As far back as 1990, two teenagers had been killed playing near the cliffs. An accident that had left the islanders traumatised. Beyond little huddles of people deep in conversation, I spotted Ange Agostini, one of the local policemen, as he was leaving the square. Instinctively, I followed him down the alleys and

47

caught up with him just as he reached his Piaggio Ape, a three-wheeled buggy parked near the harbour.

'You're going to Tristana Beach, aren't you? Can I come with you?'

Agostini turned round, mildly surprised to find me at his heels. He was a tall, bald man. An amiable Corsican, an avid reader of crime novels and a fan of the Coen brothers, whom I had introduced to my favourite Simenon books including *One Way Out*, *The Man Who Watched the Trains Go By* and *The Blue Room*.

'Get in if you like,' replied the Corsican with a shrug.

The three-wheeler crawled along the Strada Principale at between thirty and forty kilometres an hour. Agostini looked uneasy. The messages he'd received on his mobile were alarming, and led him to think it was a case of murder rather than an accident.

'I can't believe it,' he muttered. 'We don't have murders on Beaumont.'

I knew what he meant. There was no real crime on Beaumont. Virtually no assaults and very few thefts. The feeling of safety was such that people would leave their keys in their front doors or their babies in pushchairs outside shops. The local police only comprised four or five people, and the bulk of their work consisted of chatting to the inhabitants, doing their rounds and reporting faulty alarms.

4.

The road snaked its way along the rugged coast with some difficulty. It took a good twenty minutes in the Piaggio to reach Tristana Beach. As we rounded each bend, we caught the occasional hint of roof or wall, without ever seeing the huge white villas that lay hidden beyond hectares of pine forest.

All of a sudden, the landscape changed dramatically to make way for a barren plain overlooking the black sands of the shore. At this spot, Beaumont looked more like Iceland than Porquerolles.

'What the fuck?'

Ange Agostini had his foot down on the accelerator – but even travelling downhill, and on a straight stretch of road, the three-wheeler could scarcely have been nudging forty-five kilometres an hour – and pointed to where a dozen or so cars were blocking the road. When we got closer, the situation became clearer. The area was completely sealed off by cops who'd come from the mainland. Agostini parked his contraption on the roadside, and paced back and forth on the fringes of the zone now locked down behind plastic tape. I just didn't get it. How could so many men – these guys were evidently from the Serious Crime Unit in Toulon, although there was also a forensic services vehicle – have been deployed so fast on this inhospitable stretch of the coast? Where had those three police cars come from? Why had no one seen them landing at the harbour?

I mingled with the onlookers and eavesdropped on their various conversations. Little by little, I managed to piece together a rough outline of that morning's sequence of events. Around 8 a.m., a couple of Dutch students who were wild camping had discovered a woman's body. They had immediately contacted Toulon police station, who had obtained permission to use the customs division's hovercraft to send an armada of officers and three cars to the island. In order to keep a low profile, the cops had disembarked straight onto the concrete esplanade at Saragota, around ten kilometres away.

I caught up with Agostini a bit further on. He was standing on a little mound of earth by the side of the road. He seemed both devastated and a tad humiliated at not being able to access the crime scene.

'Do they know who the victim is?' I asked.

'Not yet, but they don't think it's anyone from the island.'

'Why have the cops got here so fast? And why so many? Why didn't they let anyone know?'

The Corsican stared at his phone with a distant look on his face.

'Because of the nature of the crime. And the photos those kids sent.'

'The Dutch guys took photos?'

Agostini nodded.

'They did the rounds on Twitter for a few minutes before they were taken down. But there's still a few screenshots.'

'Can I see?'

'To be honest, I wouldn't. It's not something a guy who sells books should be looking at.'

'That's crap! I could just as easily have seen them on Twitter myself.'

'OK, whatever.'

He handed me his phone and what I saw made my stomach turn. It was clearly the body of a woman. I had difficulty telling how old she was as her face seemed so horribly disfigured by her injuries. I tried to swallow, but my throat was paralysed by a vision of hell. Her corpse was naked, and looked as if it was nailed to the trunk of a gigantic eucalyptus tree. I zoomed in using the touch screen. Those weren't nails pinning the woman to the trunk. They were chisels – or maybe stonemason's tools – which had shattered her bones and been hammered deep into her flesh.

5.

Mathilde Monney was at the wheel of her convertible pickup, driving through the woods which stretched as far as Le Safranier Point. In the back of the vehicle, Bronco was barking excitedly as he watched the scenery roll by. It was a lovely day. The scent of the sea breeze mingled with the fragrance of eucalyptus and peppermint. Glints of golden-brown from the autumn sun forced their way through the leaves of the umbrella pines and evergreen oaks.

When she arrived at the rubble-stone outer wall, Mathilde got out and followed the instructions Jasper Van Wyck had given her. Near the aluminium gate, and concealed behind a stone that was darker than the others, was an entryphone. Mathilde rang the doorbell to announce her arrival. There was a crackling sound and the gate opened.

She ventured inside to discover a vast, wild estate. A dirt road ran through the wooded landscape. Sequoias, strawberry trees and groves of bay trees made the vegetation denser. Then the road twisted and turned up a steep slope, and suddenly the sea appeared along with Fawles's house: a structure composed of geometric shapes, built of ochre stone, glass and concrete.

Barely had she parked beside what she assumed to be the writer's car – a camouflage-coloured Mini Moke with a steering wheel and dashboard in lacquered wood – than the golden retriever bounded out of the pickup and made a bolt for his master, who was waiting for him in front of the door.

As he leant on his crutch, Fawles's heart leapt at seeing his companion again. Mathilde stepped a little closer. She'd imagined she was going to be confronted by some sort of caveman: a gruff old savage in rags, with long hair and a twenty-centimetre beard. But the man standing before her was freshly shaven. He had short hair, and was wearing a sky-blue linen polo shirt matching his eyes, and canvas trousers.

'Mathilde Monney,' she said, offering her hand.

'Thanks for bringing Bronco back.'

She scratched the dog's head.

'Well, I'm glad to see you're back together anyway.'

Mathilde pointed at the crutch and the plastered ankle.

'Hope that's not too serious.'

Fawles shook his head.

'Tomorrow, it'll be nothing more than a bad dream.'

She hesitated, and then said:

'You won't remember, but we've met before.'

He looked wary, and took a step back.

'I don't think so.'

'Yes, we have. It was a long time ago.'

'On what occasion?'

'I'll leave you to guess.'

6.

Fawles knew that, later on, he would tell himself this was the precise moment he ought to have pulled the plug. To have simply said what he'd agreed on with Van Wyck, 'Thanks and goodbye', and retreated inside the house. But instead he said nothing. He remained outside the door, impassive, almost mesmerised by Mathilde Monney. She was wearing a short jacquard dress, a leather biker jacket, and a pair of high-heeled sandals with delicate straps whose buckles fastened at the ankles.

He wasn't about to re-enact the opening scene of Flaubert's *Sentimental Education* – 'What he then saw was like an apparition' – but he did linger for a moment, bewitched by something elusive, something delicate yet powerful, as intense as the sun, radiating from the young woman.

His twinge of exhilaration, however, was strictly controlled. This was purely a sweet little injection of euphoria, one tiny indulgence: a quick fix of blondness, a measured shot of warm light, like the haze on a field of wheat. Not for a second did he doubt he was in command of the situation, nor that he could break the spell by snapping his fingers whenever the moment felt right.

'The poster offered a reward of 1000 euros, but I think I'll settle for an iced tea,' smiled Mathilde.

Avoiding her green eyes, Fawles explained feebly that, being unable to get around as before, he hadn't been shopping for a long time and his cupboards were empty.

'A glass of water will do,' she insisted. 'It's hot.'

Usually, he was rather good at judging people on instinct. His first impressions were often right. Now, however, he was slightly out of his depth, torn by contradictory feelings. An alarm had gone off in his head to warn him against Mathilde. But how could he resist her elusive, enigmatic appeal, and all that it promised? A soft halo, a glow as gentle and mellow as the October sun.

'Come in,' he said, caving in at last.

7.

Blue as far as the eye could see.

Mathilde was taken aback by the light flooding through the entire house. The main door opened straight into a living room which extended into a dining room and kitchen. The three rooms gave you the sensation of skimming across the waves, thanks to their enormous glazed doors which opened onto the sea. While Fawles went into the kitchen to fetch two glasses of water, Mathilde succumbed to the magic of her surroundings. She felt at ease here, soothed by the sound of the breaking surf. The sliding walls of glass eliminated the boundary between the interior and the terrace, creating a gentle sense of disorientation, to the point where you were no longer very sure of being inside or outside. In the middle of the living room was an eye-catching fireplace with a suspended hearth, while an open staircase in polished concrete led upstairs.

Mathilde had imagined this place to be a gloomy retreat, yet here again she'd got it all wrong. Fawles hadn't come to the Isle of Beaumont to bury himself away, but on the contrary to forge an intimate connection with the sky, the sea and the wind.

'Can I take a peek at the terrace?' she asked as Fawles handed her a glass.

The writer said nothing, and simply accompanied his guest onto the schist paving which seemed to stretch away into empty space. As she came closer to the edge, Mathilde felt dizzy. From this height, she could understand the architecture of the house far better. The villa was constructed right against the cliff, and in fact rose up in three separate levels. She was currently standing on the terrace of the middle one. Concrete slabs were cantilevered out from the building, each functioning in turn as base and roof. Mathilde leant over to look at the stone staircase, tracing its route to where it ended on the paved area on the lowest level. In front of her, a little pontoon granted direct access to the sea, and acted as a mooring point for a magnificent Riva Aquarama with a varnished wooden hull whose chrome fittings sparkled in the sun.

'You really get the feeling you're on the bridge of a boat.'

'Um, yeah,' said Fawles, dampening her enthusiasm. 'A boat that's going nowhere and never leaves the quay.'

For a few minutes, they busied themselves chatting about nothing in particular. Then Fawles took her back inside. Mathilde strolled around, as if she were in a museum, and wandered up to a shelf with a typewriter on it.

'I thought you'd stopped writing?' she asked, nodding at the object.

Fawles lovingly caressed the curves of the machine – a pretty almond-green model in Bakelite by Olivetti.

'It's only for decoration. Besides, it doesn't even have an ink ribbon,' he said, pressing the keys. 'And laptops already existed back in my day, you know.'

'So that's not where you wrote your—'

'No.'

She looked at him defiantly.

'I'm convinced you're still writing.'

'You're wrong. I haven't written a single word, not even a note in the margins of a book. Not even a little shopping list.'

'I don't believe you. You don't simply stop doing something overnight that used to structure every day of your life, and that—'

Fawles interrupted her wearily:

'For a second there, I thought you were different from the rest and you wouldn't bring up the subject, but I was wrong. So you're doing an investigation, are you? You're just another reporter, and you've come to churn out your little piece on "The Nathan Fawles Mystery"?'

'No, I swear I'm not.'

The writer indicated that she ought to leave.

'Time you should go now. I can't stop people making up all sorts of stuff, but the point about the Fawles mystery is precisely that there isn't one, do you get that? And you can certainly stick that in your paper.'

Mathilde made no attempt to move. Fawles hadn't changed that much since she'd last met him. He was just as she remembered – attentive, approachable, but direct. And she realised she hadn't really considered this eventuality: that Fawles might *still* be Fawles.

'But between us, don't you miss it?'

'Spending ten hours a day in front of a screen? No. I prefer spending that time in the forest or on the beach, walking with my dog.'

'I still don't believe you.'

Fawles sighed and shook his head.

'Stop making it all so sentimental. They were just books.'

'*Just* books? I can't believe you're saying that.'

'Yeah, and to be honest, largely overrated ones at that.'

Mathilde carried on with her questions:

'And now? What do you do with all your time?'

'I meditate, I drink, I cook, I drink, I swim, I drink, I go for long walks, I—'

'Do you read?'

'Oh, the odd thriller now and then, and books on the history of painting, or astronomy. I revisit a few classics, but none of that really matters.'

'Why not?'

'Well, the planet's now a blazing oven, much of the world's all blood and mayhem, and people are voting for raving lunatics, or busy frying their brains on social media. Everywhere's in total meltdown, so . . .'

'I don't see the connection.'

'So I think there are more important things than knowing why Nathan Fawles stopped writing twenty years ago.'

'But people keep reading your work.'

'What do you expect? I can't stop them. And besides, you know full well that success hangs on a misunderstanding. It was Marguerite Duras who said that, wasn't it? Or André Malraux, perhaps. Anything beyond thirty thousand copies is a misunderstanding . . .'

'Do your fans write to you too?'

'Apparently. My agent tells me he receives a lot of mail addressed to myself.'

'Do you read it?'

'You kidding or what?'

'Why?'

'Because I'm not interested. As a reader, it would never occur to me to write to an author if I liked their book. Seriously, can you imagine yourself writing to James Joyce just because you liked *Finnegans Wake*?'

'No. Firstly because I've never been able to read more than ten pages of that book, and secondly because James Joyce must have died forty years before I was born.'

Fawles shook his head.

'Listen, thanks for bringing my dog back, but you'd better go now.'

'Yes, I think so too.'

He went outside with her and walked her back to the pickup. She said goodbye to the dog, but not a word to Fawles. He watched as she manoeuvred her vehicle, hypnotised by a certain grace in her movements yet pleased to be rid of her all the same. However, just as she was about to put her foot down and drive off, he took advantage of her window being open to try to silence the little alarm that was still ringing in his head:

'You told me a bit earlier that we'd already met, a long time ago. Where was that?'

She stared into his pupils with her green eyes.

'Spring 1998, in Paris. I was fourteen. You'd come to meet patients at the Youth Care Centre. You'd even signed a copy of *Loreleï Strange* for me. A first edition in English.'

Fawles remained expressionless, as if this didn't bring anything to mind – or if it did, it was only the faintest of memories.

'I'd read *Loreleï Strange*,' continued Mathilde. 'It really helped me a lot. And I never felt the book was over-rated, or that what I learnt from reading it was part of any misunderstanding.'

GENERAL SECRETARIAT FOR THE SEA
STATE ACTION AT SEA DIVISION

PREFECTURAL ORDER No. 287/2018
Pertaining to the establishment of a temporary exclusion zone prohibiting navigation and nautical activities around the Isle of Beaumont (Département of Var), and navigation to and from the island

Squadron Vice-Admiral Édouard Lefébure
Maritime Prefect of the Mediterranean

HAVING REGARD TO Articles 131-13-1 and R610-5 of the Penal Code,

HAVING REGARD TO the Transport Code and notably Articles L5242-1 and L5242-2,

HAVING REGARD TO Decree no. 2007-1167 (amended) of 2 August 2007, pertaining to licences for, and training in, the operation of motorised pleasure boats,

HAVING REGARD TO Decree no. 2004-112 of 6 February 2004, pertaining to the organisation of State Action at Sea.

CONSIDERING THAT a criminal investigation has been opened following the discovery of a body on the Isle of Beaumont, at the location known as Tristana Beach,

CONSIDERING THAT the security forces need to be granted time to conduct their investigations on the island,

CONSIDERING THAT evidence needs to be preserved, thereby enabling the search for the truth.

ORDER

Article 1: An exclusion zone is hereby established off the coast of the Département of Var, prohibiting navigation and all nautical activities within a radius of 500 metres around and perpendicular to the shores of the Isle of Beaumont, such activities to include the transport of passengers to and from the island, with immediate effect from the issuance of this Order.

Article 2: The provisions of this Order shall not be enforceable against ships and nautical craft operating as part of public service missions.

Article 3: Any violation of this Order, as well as any decisions made in the course of its enforcement, shall render the perpetrator liable to prosecution, penalties and administrative sanctions provided for by articles L5242-1 to L5242-6-1 of the Transport Code and article R610-5 of the Penal Code.

Article 4: The Département of Var's Director of Land Management and Maritime Affairs, officials and other representatives with the authority to police navigation and nautical activities have responsibility, in accordance with their respective areas, for the execution of this Order which shall be published in the register of administrative measures enacted by the Maritime Prefecture of the Mediterranean.

Maritime Prefect of the Mediterranean,
Édouard Lefébure

4

INTERVIEWING A WRITER

Tuesday, 9 October 2018

1.

Since moving to Beaumont, I had taken to rising with the sun. After a quick shower, I'd go to meet Audibert, who'd be having his breakfast on the town square, sitting on the terrace at The Taming of the Stew or Yeast of Eden. The bookseller was unpredictable by nature. At times he'd be taciturn and withdrawn, at others forthcoming and chatty. I think, however, that he rather liked me. Or enough, at any rate, to invite me to his table every morning and offer me some tea and toast with fig jam. Mother Françoise's Preserves — flogged to tourists for the price of caviar, 'more organic than organic', 'lovingly simmered in a cauldron' and all that jazz — were one of the jewels in the island's crown.

'Good morning, Monsieur Audibert.'

He glanced up from his paper and acknowledged me with

a nervous grunt. The islanders had been left rattled, gripped by a feverish sense of unease since the day before. The discovery of a woman's body nailed to the oldest eucalyptus on the island had shocked the inhabitants. I'd learnt something else too: the tree, known locally as The Immortal, had, over the decades, become the symbol of the island's unity. The dramatic staging of the crime scene couldn't simply be a matter of chance, and the circumstances in which the victim had died had left everyone stunned beyond belief. But more than anything, what had really unsettled the residents had been the maritime prefect's decision to set up a blockade around the island to facilitate investigations. The shuttle had been confined to Saint-Julien-les-Roses, and the coastguards were under orders to go out on patrol and intercept any private boats which might attempt the crossing in one direction or the other. In practical terms, no one could leave the island and no one could land there. This measure imposed by the mainland had irritated everyone on Beaumont, who couldn't accept losing control of their collective destiny.

'This crime's a terrible blow for the island,' said Audibert furiously, closing his copy of *Var-Matin*.

It was the previous day's edition, the evening one, which had arrived on the last ferry allowed to dock. As I sat down, I glanced at the front page, plastered with the headline 'The Black Island'. A discreet nod to Hergé.

'Let's see where the investigation leads.'

'Where do you expect it to lead!' exclaimed the bookseller. 'A woman's been tortured to death and then nailed to The Immortal. That means there's a nutter loose on the island!'

I grimaced, yet I knew Audibert wasn't necessarily wrong. I wolfed down my toast and jam while skimming through the newspaper article without learning very much. Then I took out my phone in search of fresh information.

The day before, I'd spotted the Twitter account of a certain Laurent Lafaury, a journalist from the Paris area who was currently on Beaumont to visit his mother. This guy was no leading light in his field. He'd written a few online bits and pieces for the news magazines *L'Obs* and *Marianne* before becoming the community manager for a group of radio stations. His Twitter history offered a perfect example of the very worst that pseudo-journalism 2.0 could produce: smutty stories, sleazy clickbait headlines, violent spats, incitements to kill, cheap jokes, systematic retweets of distressing videos and everything that was likely to drag your intelligence into the gutter, indulging your basest instincts and pandering to your fears and fantasies. In short, the perfect little peddler of fake news and conspiracy theories, but one who always remained well hidden behind his computer screen.

Given the blockade, Lafaury now enjoyed the privilege of being the only 'journalist' present on the island. And for a few hours, he'd been making the most of his unique status: he'd taken part in the TV news on France 2 via a live link-up, and his photo had been splashed across all the news channels.

'Bloody arsehole!'

Audibert let out a stream of expletives when the journalist's profile appeared on my screen. The previous day, on the *20 Heures* news bulletin, Lafaury had managed to insinuate both that the island's residents were all hiding shameful secrets behind the 'high walls of their luxury villas', and that the code of silence would never be violated here because the Gallinaris, in true Corleone style, ruled through fear and money. If he carried on like this, Laurent Lafaury would soon turn into the bête noire of Beaumont. Media coverage of the island in such a murky context touched a raw nerve with the locals, whose quest for privacy had been so firmly embedded in their DNA for years. On Twitter, he dug himself even deeper by posting some tip-offs – apparently reliable ones – which the cops or the lawyers must have slipped his way. I wasn't in favour of this policy which, on the pretext of passing on information, compromised the confidentiality of an investigation – but I was also sufficiently curious to set my indignation aside for the time being.

Lafaury's latest tweet had been posted less than half an hour before. It was a link which sent you back to his blog. I clicked on it to access the article which offered a summary of the latest developments in the police inquiry. According to the journalist's sources, the victim was still awaiting formal identification. Whether true or not, the piece concluded with an explosive scoop: at the moment the poor soul had been nailed to the trunk of the gigantic eucalyptus, her body had been *frozen*! So, in fact, it wasn't impossible that she had died several weeks earlier.

I had to read the sentence twice to be sure I'd understood it properly. Audibert, who had stood up to look at the article over my shoulder, flopped down onto his chair, overwhelmed.

Just as Beaumont was waking to a new day, the island toppled over into a parallel world.

2.

Nathan Fawles had woken up feeling elated, something which hadn't happened for a long time. He'd had a lie-in and taken his time having breakfast. He'd then remained out on the terrace for a good hour, smoking cigarettes and listening to some old Glenn Gould records. As the fifth track was playing, he wondered – almost out loud – what could have triggered this sense of euphoria. He resisted for a moment before admitting to himself that the only thing that could explain his positive frame of mind was the memory of Mathilde Monney. A trace of her presence still lingered in the air. A gentle radiance, a soft, poetic glow, the vague hint of perfume. Something fleeting and elusive which, he knew, would evaporate before long, but which he wanted to savour down to the very last drop.

Around 11 a.m., his mood began to change. The lightness he'd felt on waking up slowly gave way to the dawning realisation that he'd probably never see Mathilde again. The realisation that, whatever he professed, his solitude could sometimes weigh heavy on him. Then, around midday, he decided to stop behaving like a child and getting all carried away like some dreamy teenager, and on the contrary to congratulate himself on sending this girl packing. He knew he mustn't crack. It simply wasn't permitted. But he did, however, allow himself to replay the film of their encounter in his mind. There was one point that had left him puzzled. A detail that wasn't a detail and that he needed to check.

He called Jasper Van Wyck in Manhattan. After several rings the literary agent answered, his voice scarcely audible. It was only 6 a.m. in New York and Jasper was still tucked up in bed. Fawles began by asking him to do some research into the articles Mathilde Monney had written for *Le Temps* in recent years.

'What exactly are you looking for?'

'I don't know. Anything you can dig up that might have something to do with me or my books, even remotely.'

'OK, but that'll take a bit of time. What else?'

'I'd like you to track down the woman who used to manage the library at the Youth Care Centre in 1998.'

'What's that?'

'A medical facility for teens run by Cochin Hospital.'

'Do you know what she's called, this librarian of yours?'

'No, I can't remember now. Can you get onto it right away?'

'OK. I'll call you back as soon as I've found anything.'

Fawles hung up and went into the kitchen to make himself a coffee. As he leisurely sipped his espresso, he tried to recollect whatever he could. Located near Port-Royal in the south of Paris, the Youth Care Centre took charge of adolescents, primarily those affected by eating disorders, depression, school phobia and anxiety. Some of them would be admitted as in-patients, while others were treated within the day clinic. Fawles had gone there two or three times to give talks to the young residents, of whom the majority were girls. There had been a talk, and a Q&A session, and he'd also led a small writing workshop. He could no longer remember their names or their faces, but he had retained a very positive overall impression. Attentive readers, a rewarding discussion and questions that often hit the nail on the head. He was finishing his cup when the phone rang. Jasper hadn't wasted any time.

'I found the library manager easily, thanks to LinkedIn. Her name's Sabina Benoit.'

'That's her. It's come back to me now.'

'She stayed at the Youth Care Centre until 2012. Since then she's been working out in the provinces, with the Library for All network. According to the latest information I could find online, she's currently in Dordogne, in a place called Trélissac. Do you want her number?'

Fawles noted her contact details and called Sabina Benoit at once. The librarian was both surprised and delighted to hear his voice on the phone. Fawles recalled her general appearance better than her face. A tall, energetic woman with short dark hair and an infectious warmth. He'd met her at the Paris Book Fair, and let himself be talked into coming to discuss writing with her patients.

'I'm in the middle of working on my memoirs,' he began. 'And I'll need a—'

'Your memoirs? Do you really think I'm going to buy that, Nathan?' she interrupted, laughing.

Better to come clean after all.

'I'm looking for some information about a patient at the Youth Care Centre. A young girl who'd have been at one of my talks. A certain Mathilde Monney.'

'It doesn't ring a bell,' replied Sabina after a moment's thought. 'But my memory's fading, the older I get.'

'We're kind of all in the same boat. I'm trying to find out why Mathilde Monney was admitted.'

'I don't have access to that kind of information these days, and even if—'

'Oh, come on, Sabina, surely you've still got some contacts? Do it for me. Just a little favour. Please. It's really important.'

'I'll try, but I can't promise anything.'

Fawles hung up and went off to ferret through his book-case. It was a good while before he finally laid his hands on a copy of *Loreleï Strange*. It was a first edition. The first that had gone on sale in bookshops, back in autumn 1993. He wiped the dust off the cover with the palm of his hand. It featured his favourite painting, *Young Acrobat on a Ball*, a sublime Picasso from the artist's Rose Period. It was Fawles himself who, at the time, had cobbled this cover together, by making a collage that he'd submitted to the publisher. The latter had had so little faith in the book that he'd let him do what he wanted.

The initial print run of *Loreleï* had been limited to five thou-sand copies. The novel hadn't received any press coverage, and you couldn't exactly say that booksellers had gone out of their way to champion it – even if they'd ended up following the crowd later on. No, this book owed its salvation purely to the enthusiastic word of mouth of its readers. Mostly young girls, like the Mathilde Monney of the time, who had iden-tified with the main character – and, admittedly, the book's narrative lent itself rather well to such a response. It told the story of Loreleï, a young inmate in a psychiatric institution, and the various people she encountered in the course of a weekend. This set-up was the pretext for describing an entire gallery of characters living in the hospital.

Little by little, the novel had hauled itself up through the sales rankings, eventually reaching the coveted status of a lit-erary phenomenon. Those who'd snubbed it at the beginning hurried to jump on the bandwagon. The book was read by the young, the old, the chattering classes, teachers, pupils, people who read a lot, people who didn't read at all. Everyone began to have an opinion on *Loreleï Strange* and the book was quoted as saying things it never actually said. That was it, the great misunderstanding, right there. Over the years, the movement had grown and *Loreleï* had become a sort of classic of mainstream literature. People had written theses about it, and you were as likely to find it in bookshops and airports as you were in the books section at supermarkets. Sometimes even on the self-help shelf, which infuriated its author. And what was bound to happen did happen: even before he'd stopped writing, Fawles's sense of being imprisoned by his own book became so strong that he began to hate the novel, and couldn't bear anyone discussing it with him any longer.

The chiming of the doorbell pulled the writer back into the present. He replaced the book and glanced at the security camera. It was Dr Sicard, who'd finally come to remove his cast. He'd almost forgotten! The cavalry was here.

3.

The Tristana Beach murder.

Customers coming into the bookshop, tourists, locals passing through the square: that was practically all anyone could talk about. I'd seen more than my fair share of gawkers at The Scarlet Rose since early afternoon. Very few bona fide purchasers, but instead people who simply drifted into the shop for a brief chat – some to ward off their fears, others just to feed their morbid curiosity.

I'd set up my MacBook on the welcome desk. The shop's internet connection was pretty fast, but it frequently went down, forcing me to go back up to the first floor each time to restart the router. My browser was open at Laurent Lafaury's Twitter account – he had just updated his blog that very second.

According to his information, the cops had managed to identify the victim. A woman aged thirty-eight. A certain Apolline Chapuis, a wine dealer from the Chartrons district of Bordeaux. Initial witness statements indicated she had been on the quayside in Saint-Julien-les-Roses on 20 August. A few passengers had seen her on the ferry that day, but detectives were still trying to find out why she had come to the island. One of their theories was that someone had lured Apolline to Beaumont, then held her captive before killing her and preserving her body in a cold store or a freezer. The journalist's article concluded with a crazy rumour: there was to be a massive wave of police raids on every house on the island, to identify where the victim had been kept prisoner.

I checked the post office calendar – illustrated with the iconic portrait of Arthur Rimbaud by Carjat – which Audibert had stuck up behind the screen of his PC. If the journalist's sources were to be believed, Apolline had landed on the island three weeks before me. During those last days of August, when torrential rain had lashed down on the Mediterranean.

Through sheer force of habit, I typed her name into the search engine.

In just a few clicks, I found myself on the site that belonged to Apolline's company. The young woman wasn't exactly a 'wine dealer', as Lafaury had claimed. She did indeed work in the wine industry, but her area was more sales and marketing. Her small business was very active in overseas markets, dealing with the sale of prestigious wines to hotels and restaurants, as well as curating ready-to-use wine cellars for wealthy individuals. Her CV was available via the 'About us' tab and spelt out the key milestones in the company founder's career. Born in Paris into a family who owned shares in several vineyards around Bordeaux, she had studied for a master's in 'Vine and Wine Law' from the University of Bordeaux IV, followed by a national diploma in oenology awarded by Montpellier's French National Institute of Higher Education in Agricultural Sciences. Apolline had then worked in London and Hong Kong before setting up her little consultancy firm. Her photo, in black and white, suggested she had a pleasing appearance – that is, for those who liked tall blondes who looked a bit sad.

What had she come to the island for? Was it to do with her work? That was quite possible. Grapevines were a long-established feature on Beaumont. As on Porquerolles, the vineyards were originally intended to act as a firebreak. Today, several wine-growing estates on the island produced a perfectly decent Côtes de Provence. The biggest winery – the pride of Beaumont, and the source of its fame – belonged to the Gallinaris. In the early 2000s, the Corsican branch of the family had planted some rare varieties of vine in soil rich in clay and limestone. While at first everyone thought they were utterly insane, their white wine – the celebrated Terra dei Pini, of which they produced twenty thousand bottles a year – had now gained a stellar reputation, featuring on the menus of the greatest restaurants in the world. I'd been fortunate enough to taste this divine nectar several times since my arrival. It was a dry white, fine and fruity, with a subtle hint of flowers and bergamot. The entire production process conformed to biodynamic principles, and made the most of the island's mild climate.

I buried my head back in the screen to read Lafaury's article again. For the first time in my life, I felt like a detective in a real whodunnit. And, as with each time I experienced something interesting, I wanted to crystallise it by writing a novel. Mysterious images, disturbing ones, were already springing to life in my imagination: a Mediterranean island paralysed by a blockade, the frozen corpse of a young woman, a famous writer locked away inside his house for twenty years . . .

I started a new document on my computer and began typing the opening lines of my narrative:

Chapter 1.
Tuesday, 11 September 2018
The wind was slapping at the sails in a dazzling sky.
The dinghy had left the Var coast a little after 1 p.m., and was now flying along at a speed of five knots towards the Isle of Beaumont. Sitting near the helm, just beside the skipper, I was bewitched by the spell of the breeze from the sea, completely transfixed as I gazed at the dusting of gold that glittered across the Mediterranean.

4.

The sun was setting beyond the horizon, streaking the sky with splashes of orange. Fawles was hobbling along as he returned from a walk with his dog. He'd tried to be too clever by half in ignoring the doctor's advice. As soon as Sicard had freed him from his cast, he'd gone rushing out with Bronco, without carrying a stick or taking precautions of any kind. And now he was paying dearly for it: he was short of breath, his ankle felt like lead and all of his muscles were aching.

The moment he arrived back in his living room, Fawles sank into the sofa facing the sea and swallowed an anti-inflammatory pill. He closed his eyes for a few moments, trying to catch his breath while the golden retriever licked his hands. He'd almost nodded off when the doorbell chimed and made him sit up again.

The writer leant on the edge of the sofa to get up, and limped over to the security camera. Mathilde Monney's luminous face appeared on the screen.

Nathan froze. What on earth was the woman doing here? A repeat visit, in his mind, felt both promising and ominous at the same time. Coming back to see him meant Mathilde Monney had some ulterior motive. *What should he do? Refuse to answer?* It was a means of warding off danger in the short term, certainly, but it wouldn't let him work out the *nature* of the threat.

Fawles unlocked the front gate without even speaking into the entryphone. His heart had stopped racing and, once he'd got over the initial surprise, he was determined to defuse the situation. He was well up to the task of confronting Mathilde. He had to dissuade her from poking her nose into his affairs, and that was what he was about to do. But gently.

Like the previous day, he went outside to wait for her on the doorstep. He leant against the doorframe, with Bronco at his feet, and watched her pickup as it drew closer, whipping up clouds of dust. The young woman stopped in front of the steps and applied the handbrake. She slammed the door and stood facing him for a moment. She was wearing a short-sleeved dress in a flowery print over a rib-knit roll-neck jumper. The last few rays of sunlight lent a golden sheen to her mustard leather high-heeled boots.

From the way she looked at him, Fawles was convinced of two things. The first: Mathilde Monney didn't just happen to be on the island *by chance*. Her sole reason for being on Beaumont was to discover his secret. The second: Mathilde didn't have the faintest idea what that secret might be.

'I see they've taken your plaster off! Could you come and give me a hand?' she called out as she began to unload the brown paper bags piled up in the back of the vehicle.

'What's all this?'

'I've been shopping for you. Your cupboards are empty. You told me so, yesterday.'

Fawles stubbornly remained where he was.

'I don't need a home help. I can do my own shopping just fine.'

From where he was standing, he could smell Mathilde's perfume. Crystalline scents of mint, citrus and freshly washed linen, mingling with those of the forest.

'Ah! Don't you go thinking it's a free service. I simply want to check out that story. Well, are you helping or not?'

'What story?' asked Fawles, feebly grabbing the remaining bags.

'That story about the blanquette de veau.'

Fawles thought he had misheard, but Mathilde went on to explain:

'In your final interview, you bragged you could make a divine blanquette. Well, that's lucky – it's one of my favourites!'

'I thought you were more the vegetarian type.'

'Not in the least. I've bought you all the ingredients. Now you've no excuse not to invite me to dinner.'

Fawles realised she wasn't joking. He hadn't seen this coming, but convinced himself he was still calling the shots and nodded at Mathilde to go inside.

Making herself at home, the young woman set the bags down on the living room table, hung her leather jacket on the coat rack and opened a bottle of Corona which she went off to sip peacefully on the terrace while admiring the sunset.

Left alone in the kitchen, Fawles set about cooking with a fake air of nonchalance.

That whole blanquette thing was a piece of bullshit. A wisecrack he'd whipped out in response to a journalist's question. Whenever he was quizzed about his private life, he applied Italo Calvino's principle: either you refuse to answer or you lie. But he wasn't about to duck out of it. He selected the ingredients he needed and put the rest of the food away, trying to avoid leaning on his painful leg. He searched through his cupboard and found a cooking pot with an enamelled base which he hadn't used for ages, and put some olive oil on to heat. Then he took out a chopping board and began slicing up the chunks of veal cushion and shank, and minced some garlic and parsley which he stirred into the meat as it was browning. He added a spoonful of flour and a large glass of white wine before covering everything with hot stock. From memory, he now had to leave it to simmer for a good hour.

He took a peek into the other rooms. Night had fallen and Mathilde had come back inside to warm herself up. She'd put an old record by The Yardbirds on the turntable and was nosing around the bookcase. Fawles chose a Saint-Julien from the wine cooler next to the fridge, which he slowly decanted into a carafe before returning to join Mathilde in the living room.

'It's a bit chilly in here,' she said. 'I wouldn't say no to a nice little fire.'

'Yes, of course.'

Fawles went over to the metal racks that functioned as log holders. He gathered some kindling and some logs, and lit a fire in the suspended hearth in the centre of the room.

Mathilde carried on wandering around. She half opened the cabinet fixed to the wall beside a pile of firewood and discovered the shotgun kept inside.

'Ah, so it's not a myth: you really *do* shoot at the people who turn up to hassle you?'

'Yeah. And count yourself lucky you're not one of them.'

She examined the weapon closely. The butt and the stock were in waxed walnut, while the barrel was made of polished steel. Between the bluish glints on the body of the gun, amid the ornate arabesques, a face that looked like the Devil glared at her menacingly.

'Is that Satan?' she asked.

'No, it's the kulshedra: a horned female dragon from Albanian folklore.'

'Delightful.'

He grazed her shoulder as he led her away from the log racks, taking her over to the fireplace where he poured her a glass of wine. They toasted each other and enjoyed the Saint-Julien in silence.

'A Château Gruaud Larose 1982. Well, you're clearly not messing me around,' she said, approvingly.

She sat down in the leather armchair near the sofa, lit a cigarette and played with Bronco. Fawles went back into the kitchen, checked his blanquette and mixed in some pitted olives and mushrooms. He made some rice, and laid out two plates and cutlery in the dining room. When the veal had finished cooking, he added the juice of a lemon whisked with an egg yolk to the pot.

'Dinner's ready!' he shouted as he carried out his dish.

Before joining him, she placed another record on the turntable: the music from the film *The Old Gun*. Fawles watched her clicking her fingers to the rhythm of François de Roubaix's melody while Bronco scampered around her. Such a beautiful scene. Mathilde was beautiful. It would have been easy to surrender himself to the moment, but he knew it was all just a cunning mind game between two people, each of whom believed they could outmanoeuvre the other. Fawles suspected this game would not be without its consequences. He had taken the risk of letting the fox into the henhouse. Never had anyone been so close to the secret he'd been hiding for twenty years.

The blanquette had turned out well. They certainly ate heartily, in any case. Fawles was no longer in the habit of talking very much, but the dinner was still an upbeat affair thanks to Mathilde who was full of humour and high spirits, and had a theory for everything. Then, at a certain moment, something changed in her expression. The spark was still there – but she became more serious, and her laughter subsided.

'Seeing it's your birthday, I've brought you a present.'

'I was born in June, so it's not really my birthday.'

'OK, so I might be a bit early, or a bit late. It doesn't

matter. Seeing as you're a novelist, you're going to like this.'

'I'm not a novelist. Not now.'

'I think being a novelist is like being Président de la République. It's a title you hang on to, even when you're no longer in office.'

'That's up for debate, but if you say so.'

She chose a different line of attack.

'Novelists are the biggest liars in history, aren't they?'

'No, that would be politicians. And historians. And journalists. But not novelists.'

'Yes they are! When you claim your novels are all about life, you're lying. Life's too complex to be reduced to an equation, or imprisoned in the pages of a book. It's much deeper than maths or fiction. A novel is fiction. And fiction is technically lies.'

'It's quite the opposite. Philip Roth put it rather well when he said that fiction "provides the storyteller with the lie through which to expose his unspeakable truth".'

'Yes, but—'

Suddenly Fawles had had enough.

'We're not going to settle the matter tonight. So what's my present, then?'

'I thought you didn't want one.'

'Christ, you're a frigging pain in the ass, no kidding!'

'My present is a story.'

'What story?'

Still holding her glass of wine, Mathilde had left the table and returned to sit in the armchair.

'I'm going to *tell* you a story. And when I've finished it, you'll have no choice but to sit down at your typewriter and start writing again.'

Fawles shook his head.

'No way.'

'Wanna bet?'

'I'm not betting a damn thing.'

'Are you scared?'

'Not of you, anyhow. There's nothing whatsoever that would make me go back to writing, and I don't see how your story would make a blind bit of difference.'

'Because it concerns you. And because it's a story that needs an epilogue.'

'I'm not sure I want to hear it.'

'I'm going to share it with you anyway.'

Without moving from her chair, she held out her empty glass to Fawles. He took the Saint-Julien, got up to refill Mathilde's glass and sank back into the sofa. He'd realised things were about to get serious, and everything else had been nothing but meaningless babble. A prelude to their real face-off.

Mathilde launched into her tale:

'The story begins in Oceania at the very start of the 2000s. A young couple from the Paris region, Apolline Chapuis and Karim Amrani, land in Hawaii after flying for fifteen hours to spend a holiday there.'

5

THE BEARER OF A STORY

2000

The story begins in Oceania at the very start of the 2000s.

A young couple from the Paris region, Apolline Chapuis and Karim Amrani, landed in Hawaii after flying for fifteen hours for a week's holiday. Barely had they arrived than they emptied the minibar in their hotel room and sank into a deep sleep. The next day, and the day after, they made the most of the volcanic island of Maui and its charms. They went hiking through nature, wild and unspoilt, and gazed in wonder at little waterfalls and vast flower-filled landscapes while smoking a joint or two. They shagged on smooth, silky beaches and hired a private boat to go whale-watching off the coast at Lahaina. On the third day, while they were treating themselves to a beginner's lesson in scuba diving, their camera fell into the ocean.

The two expert divers who were with them tried unsuccessfully to recover it. Apolline and Karim simply had to come to terms with the fact: they had lost their holiday photos. Which they promptly forgot about that very evening, over a good dozen cocktails in one of the many bars along the beach.

2015

But life holds its share of surprises.

Many years later, nine thousand kilometres away, Eleanor Farago, an American businesswoman, glimpsed an object caught on a reef while she was out jogging on Baishawan Beach in Kenting, a region in the south of Taiwan.

It was now spring 2015. It was 7 a.m. Miss Farago, who worked for an international hotel chain, was on a tour of Asia to visit a few establishments that were part of her group. On the last morning of her stay, before catching her flight back to New York, she'd gone running at 'Baisha', the Côte d'Azur of Taiwan. Surrounded by hills, the beach was blessed with fine, golden sand and translucent water, along with several reefs plunging into the sea. It was there that Eleanor spotted this mysterious object. She ran over, scrambled up two rocks, bent down to dislodge the item and examined it. It was a waterproof case containing a camera, a PowerShot made by Canon.

She wasn't to know yet (and to tell the truth, she never would), but the camera belonging to the young French couple had been drifting for fifteen years, its course determined purely by random obstacles and ocean currents, over a distance of almost ten thousand kilometres. Intrigued, Eleanor grabbed the object and, when she got back to the hotel, slipped it inside a cloth pouch in her hand luggage. A few hours later, she boarded her plane at Taipei Airport.

Her Delta Air Lines flight, which left at 12.35, made a stop-over in San Francisco and finally touched down in New York, at JFK Airport, at 23.08, more than three hours late. Exasperated by her journey, and desperate to get home, she left several items behind in her seat pocket – including the camera.

The team responsible for cleaning the plane recovered the pouch and deposited it with the Lost and Found service at JFK Airport. Three weeks later, one of its employees came across Miss Farago's plane ticket. By cross-checking some details, he managed to leave her a message on her answer-phone and also send her an email, but Eleanor Farago never responded to either.

As per standard procedure, the Lost and Found service held on to the camera for ninety days. At the end of this period, it was sold on, along with thousands of other objects, to a company in Alabama which had been dealing in unclaimed baggage purchased from American airlines for decades.

And so, in the early autumn of 2015, the camera found itself stored away on the shelves of the Unclaimed Baggage Center. This place was like nowhere else. It had all started in the 1970s, in Scottsboro, a small town in Jackson County, two hundred kilometres to the north-west of Atlanta. A modest family-run concern had come up with the idea of signing contracts with airlines to sell on lost luggage whose owners had never come forward. The business had done so well that, over the years, the firm had become a veritable institution.

In 2015, the Center's warehouses stretched across nearly four thousand square metres. Each and every day, articulated lorries brought more than seven thousand new items here from various airports across the US – all to this little town lost in the middle of nowhere. The curious came flooding in from all over the country and even beyond: each year a million visitors now descended on this place which resembled as much a discount supermarket as it did a gallery of the weird and wonderful. Four entire floors were stacked high with clothes, computers, tablets, headphones, musical instruments and watches. A little museum had even been created within the Center to display the most bizarre items collected over the years, including an eighteenth-century Italian violin, an Egyptian funerary mask, a 5.8 carat diamond and an urn containing someone's ashes . . .

So it was that our Canon PowerShot landed on the shelves of this curious store. Protected by its fabric pouch, it remained there, piled up with other cameras, from September 2015 to December 2017.

2017

During the Christmas holidays that year, Scottie Malone, who was forty-four, and his eleven-year-old daughter Billie, who both lived in Scottsboro, found themselves wandering down the aisles at the Unclaimed Baggage Center. The store's prices were sometimes eighty per cent lower than those of brand-new items, and Scottie was hardly made of money. He ran a small business on the road leading to Guntersville Lake, a garage where he repaired both cars and boats.

Ever since his wife had left, he'd been trying to bring up his daughter as best he could. Julia had done a runner one winter's day, three years earlier. Arriving home in the evening, he'd found a note on the kitchen table coldly announcing the news. It had hurt, of course, and the wound was still raw, even now, but he hadn't been all that surprised. To tell the truth, he'd always known his wife would leave one day. It's written somewhere, on a page in the Book of Destiny, that the most beautiful roses live haunted by the fear of fading. And this fear sometimes makes them carry out irreparable acts.

'Can I get a paintbox for Christmas, Papa? Please?' asked Billie.

Scottie nodded to indicate his approval. They went up to the top floor where the books were shelved, along with anything to do with stationery. They rooted around for a good quarter of an hour and finally dug out a pretty set of gouache paint tubes, some oil pastels and two little blank canvases. The joy on his daughter's face warmed Scottie's heart. He decided to treat himself too: a copy of *The Poet* by Michael Connelly, marked down to 99 cents. It was Julia who had shown him the magical power of reading. It was she who, for a long time, had been recommending books he would probably like, such as thrillers, historical novels and tales of adventure. It wasn't always easy getting into the narrative, but once you'd found the right book – the one that was made for you, the one where you savoured all the details, every dialogue, what the characters were thinking – it was the best form of escape. Yes, it was better than anything, it really was. Better than Netflix, better than a Hawks basketball match, and better than all those moronic videos circulating on social media which transformed you into a zombie.

As they were queuing at the checkouts, Scottie's eye fell on a basket containing a jumble of discounted items. He rummaged around in the big wire-mesh bin and, from among a motley assortment of objects, fished out a bulging cloth pouch. It contained an old-style compact camera, priced at $4.99. After a moment's thought, he gave in to temptation. He loved tinkering around with stuff, patching back together whatever came to hand. Each time it turned into a formidable challenge which he felt duty bound to overcome. Because, whenever he was fixing some old, clapped-out object to get it working again, it always felt slightly as though he were mending his own life too.

When they arrived home, Scottie and Billie decided by mutual agreement that, although it was only Saturday 23 December, they could open their presents without waiting for Christmas Day. That would give them the rest of the weekend to enjoy them, as Scottie had to work in the garage on Monday. It was cold that year. Scottie made his daughter a cup of hot chocolate with mini marshmallows which bobbed around like foam on top. Billie put on some music and spent the afternoon painting while her father read his thriller and sipped a cold beer.

It was only when evening came – while Billie was busy making macaroni cheese – that Scottie opened the pouch containing the camera. On examining the condition of the waterproof case, he guessed the device had probably been in the water for several years. He needed a serrated knife to force open the protective cover. The camera had stopped working, but, after several attempts, he managed to extract its memory card which didn't appear to be damaged. He connected it to his computer and succeeded in copying over the photos stored on it.

Scottie felt a slight frisson as he viewed the snaps. The sensation of entering the private lives of people he didn't know made him feel uneasy as much as it piqued his curiosity. There were around forty images. The last few pictures featured a decadent young couple in an idyllic setting: beaches, turquoise water, lush vegetation, underwater shots of brightly coloured fish. On one of the snaps, the couple were posing outside a hotel. A photo snatched on the fly, the camera above their heads, a selfie before its time with the Aumakua Hotel in the background. In just a few clicks, Scottie found it on the internet: a luxury hotel in Hawaii.

Probably where the camera was lost. It must have fallen into the ocean.

Scottie scratched his head. There were other photos on the memory card. The dates stamped on them indicated they'd been taken a few weeks *before* the ones in Hawaii, but they didn't really fit with the later snaps. These were different people, most probably in a different country and in a different context. Who had this camera belonged to? Scottie left his screen to go and have dinner with this question preying on his mind.

As he'd promised his daughter he would, they spent the evening watching 'scary Christmas movies' – *Gremlins* and *The Nightmare Before Christmas*, to be precise.

Slumped in front of the TV, Scottie carried on musing over what he'd found. He drank another beer, then another, and sank deep into the sofa, fast asleep.

★

When he awoke the next day, it was almost 10 a.m. He was slightly ashamed of having slept so long, and discovered his daughter busy 'working' at her computer.

'Shall I make you a coffee, Papa?'

'You know you're not allowed to go online on your own!' he said angrily.

Feeling hurt at being told off, Billie shrugged and went off to sulk in the kitchen.

Scottie noticed a folded old bit of paper lying on the desk, beside the computer. It looked like an e-ticket for a flight.

'Where did you find that?'

'In the little cloth bag,' replied Billie, poking her head back into the room.

Scottie screwed up his eyes, trying to read the details printed on the ticket. It was a Delta Air Lines flight which, on 12 May 2015, had left Taipei bound for New York. The passenger was a certain Eleanor Farago. Scottie looked puzzled. This was all getting harder and harder to figure out.

'Listen, I know exactly what happened! You were out for the count, so I had time to think about it!' said Billie triumphantly.

She sat down at the computer and began printing out the world map she had just downloaded from the internet. Then, using a pen, she highlighted a tiny area in the middle of the Pacific.

'The camera was lost in Hawaii in 2000 by the couple who were scuba diving,' she began, scrolling through the last few photos they'd found on the device.

'Yup, I agree with you so far,' said her father as he put on his glasses.

Billie pointed to the plane ticket as she drew a long arrow

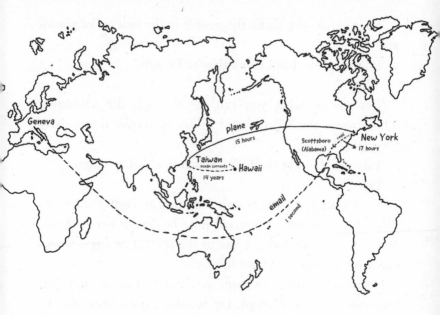

across the ocean, from Hawaii towards Taiwan.

'Then the camera drifted, and was carried by the current to the Taiwanese coast, where it was found in 2015 by this woman, this Miss Farago.'

'Who then presumably forgot it in the plane when she got back to the US?'

'Affirmative,' replied Billie, nodding. 'And that's how it got all the way here, to us.'

Taking great care, she finished her diagram with a new arrow leading to New York and then added a dotted line to their little town.

Scottie was impressed by his daughter's powers of deduction. Billie had put together a version of the jigsaw that was practically complete. Only one piece of the puzzle was still missing:

'So, who do you think the people in the first set of photos are?'

'I don't know, but I think they're French.'

'Why?'

'Because of what you can see through the windows. Those roofs, that's Paris,' said Billie. 'And over there, that's the Eiffel Tower.'

'I always thought the Eiffel Tower was in Las Vegas.'

'Papa!'

'I'm kidding,' replied Scottie, nodding and reflecting wistfully that he'd once promised Julia he'd take her to Paris, and that promise had got lost in the torrent of days, weeks and years that eroded your life away.

He looked at the Paris snaps over and over again, and then the ones taken in Hawaii. He wouldn't have been able to say precisely why, but he was mesmerised by this series of images. As if some tragedy were brewing behind these two sequences. As if there were some mystery to solve, worthy of any plot in those thrillers he devoured with such passion.

What could he do with these photos? There was no reason to pass them on to the police, but a little voice in his head told him he had to show them to someone. Maybe a journalist? And preferably a French journalist. But Scotty didn't speak a word of French.

His daughter handed him a cup of black coffee.

'Thanks.'

Then they both sat down at the computer. Over the next hour, through trial and error and by typing keywords into search engines, they found someone who matched the profile they had specified: a French journalist who had completed part of her studies in New York, obtaining a Master of

Science from Columbia University. She'd then gone back to Europe and was currently working for a Swiss daily.

Billie found her contact details on the newspaper's website, and father and daughter composed an email in which they outlined what they had discovered, and why they felt they were dealing with a mystery. To lend added weight to their words, they attached a selection of photos found on the camera. Then they sent off their note, like a message in a bottle.

The journalist was called Mathilde Monney.

THE ANGEL WITH
GOLDEN HAIR

AN EXCERPT FROM THE PROGRAMME
BOUILLON DE CULTURE

Broadcast on France 2 on
20 November 1998

[A chic, minimalist set: cream-coloured drop curtains, antique columns, a fake bookcase giving the illusion of being sculpted in marble. The guests are seated in black leather armchairs, arranged in a circle around a coffee table. With his half-moon glasses perched on his nose, and dressed in a tweed jacket, iconic presenter Bernard Pivot steals a glance at his index cards before asking each question.]

Bernard Pivot: We're running behind, but before we go, Nathan Fawles, you're not escaping our traditional quick-fire quiz! First question: what's your favourite word?

Nathan Fawles: Light!

Pivot: The word you hate most?

Fawles: Voyeurism. It sounds as ugly as what it means.

Pivot: Your favourite drug?

Fawles: Japanese whisky. Especially Bara No Niwa – their distillery was destroyed in the 1980s, and they've—

Pivot: Whoa! Whoa! We can't go plugging a whisky brand on a public service channel! Next question: your favourite sound?

Fawles: Silence.

Pivot: And the sound or noise you hate?

Fawles: Silence.

Pivot: Ah! Your favourite swear word, curse or expletive?

Fawles: Bastard.

Pivot: That's not very literary, is it!

Fawles: I've never understood what's 'literary' and what isn't.

Pivot: Man or woman to feature on a new banknote?

Fawles: Alexandre Dumas *fils*, who became very wealthy before losing the whole lot, and reminded us quite rightly that money is a good servant, but a bad master.

Pivot: The plant, tree or animal you'd like to be reborn as?

Fawles: A dog, because they're often more humane than humans are. Do you know the story of Levinas and his dog?

Pivot: No, but I'm sure you'll come and tell us another time. Last question: if God does exist, what would you like to hear him say to you after you die, Nathan Fawles?

Fawles: 'You've not exactly been a saint, Fawles . . . But then again, neither have I!'

Pivot: 'Thanks for being with us, goodnight everyone and see you next week.'

[Closing credits music: The Night Has a Thousand Eyes*, played on the saxophone by Sonny Rollins.]*

6

WRITERS AND THEIR TIME OFF

Wednesday, 10 October 2018

1.

It wasn't light yet. Fawles came gingerly down the stairs, his dog at his heels. In the dining room, the table was still a mess, its unvarnished wood cluttered with the remains of the previous evening's meal. His eyelids were heavy and his mind was a complete blur. Fawles set to work tidying the room, moving around on autopilot in a ballet of toing and froing between the living room and the kitchen.

When he had finished, he fed Bronco and brewed himself a large pot of coffee. After the night he'd just been through, he felt lost, adrift in a fog, and wished he could simply inject himself with some caffeine – straight into his veins – to help find his way through.

Clasping a scalding hot mug, Fawles went out to the terrace, shivering as he did so. Streaks of rosy pink, constantly shifting and changing, merged into the midnight blue of a celestial canvas. The mistral had been blowing all night and was still sweeping along the coast. The air was dry and icy-cold, as if, in merely a few hours, the season had changed abruptly from summer to winter. The writer zipped up the neck of his jumper and sat down at a table positioned in an alcove. A little cocoon, sheltered from the wind and coated in whitewash, which served as a patio.

Nathan was deep in thought. He replayed the film of Mathilde's story, trying to reassemble the segments in a logical order. So the journalist had been contacted via email by some redneck from Alabama, who had bought an old camera in a superstore which recycled items left behind in planes. The camera had probably been lost in 2000 by two French tourists in the Pacific and had turned up again fifteen years later on a beach in Taiwan. It contained several photos that, from what Mathilde had implied, hinted at the possibility of some kind of tragic event.

'Well, what was in those snaps?' Fawles had asked when the young woman was taking a break from telling her story.

She had given him a long, hard stare with those sparkling eyes.

'That's all for tonight, Nathan. You'll hear the rest of the story tomorrow. Shall we arrange to meet in the afternoon? At Pine Cove?'

At first he'd thought she was joking, but the little bitch had drained her glass of Saint-Julien and risen from her chair.

'You taking the piss or what?'

But she'd already slipped on her leather jacket, picked up the keys she'd left in the little bowl in the hall and given Bronco a gentle scratch on the head.

'Thanks for the blanquette and the wine. Have you never thought of doing evening meals? You'd be a runaway success, I'm sure.'

And she had left the house feeling rather smug, refusing to say any more.

You'll hear the rest of the story tomorrow . . .

That had sent him flying into a rage. Who the hell did she think she was, this trashy cut-price Scheherazade? So she wanted to create her own little cliffhanger, did she? Taking him on at his own game, proving that she too was perfectly capable of giving those who listened to her stories a few sleepless nights?

Pretentious little so-and-so . . . Fawles swallowed a last mouthful of coffee and made an effort to calm down again. The epic journey of the digital camera was far from being uninteresting. It had a certain potential as a novel, even if, for the moment, he couldn't quite see where it might lead. Crucially, he couldn't understand why Mathilde had claimed that the story concerned him, *him* in particular. He had never set foot in Hawaii nor Taiwan, let alone Alabama. If the story was linked to him, it could therefore only be in relation to what was in the photos, but neither of the names she had mentioned – Apolline Chapuis and Karim Amrani – meant anything to him.

And yet he had a strong hunch that none of this was insignificant. Behind these theatricals something was afoot – something that was far more serious than a simple game of literary seduction. What was this girl after, for God's sake? In the short term, at any rate, she'd pulled it off, as he hadn't slept a wink all night. He'd been tricked, like a rookie soldier. Worse: he was now reacting precisely as she expected he would.

Fuck it . . . He couldn't just sit back and put up with this. Not any longer. He had to act – to try to find out more about this girl before the trap she was setting closed around him. He rubbed his frozen hands against each other, his face strained and taut. It was all very well, wanting to make inquiries, but he hadn't the faintest idea of how he might go about it. Without internet access, he couldn't conduct an investigation while staying locked up at home, and his ankle, which was still stiff, swollen and painful, remained a real handicap. Once again, his first instinct was to call Jasper Van Wyck. But Jasper was a long way off. He could perhaps do some online research on his behalf, but he couldn't really act as the armed wing of Fawles's counterattack against Mathilde. Fawles considered the problem from every possible angle, but – no matter which way he looked at it – he was finally forced to admit he'd only get through his predicament by asking for help. He needed someone resourceful. Someone capable of taking risks. Someone who'd be wholly committed to his cause and wouldn't ask a million questions.

One name clearly stood out in his mind. He rose from his chair and went back into the living room to make a call.

2.

I was huddled up under the bedclothes, shivering from head to toe. The temperature must have dropped by ten degrees since the previous day. As I was going to bed, I'd remembered to turn on the cast-iron radiator in my tiny room, yet it remained frustratingly cold to the touch.

From beneath my covers I could see dawn breaking through the window, but for the first time since being here I was finding it tough to get up. The discovery of Apolline Chapuis's body and the blockade ordered by the prefecture had changed Beaumont completely. In barely a couple of days, this little Mediterranean paradise had been brutally transformed into one gigantic crime scene.

So that put an end to it – to the spirit of friendship, the pleasures of pre-lunch drinks and the usual bonhomie among the locals. Even the hot weather had buggered off. From now on, suspicion lurked everywhere. And the tension had cranked up yet another notch today, when one of the national weeklies had splashed 'The Isle of Beaumont's Dark Secrets' across its front page. As often happens with this kind of special edition thrown together at the last minute, nothing was true. The articles inside were a tissue of lies, of unverified facts and misleading simplification which fed lurid headlines and subheads. Beaumont was at times portrayed as a haven for millionaires – that is, when it wasn't apparently a refuge for billionaires – and at others as a hideaway for fanatical separatists who made the Tamil Tigers look like the Care Bears. The addition of the Gallinaris, the island's highly discreet owners, simply fuelled these fantasies even more. It was as if it had taken this tragedy for all of France to realise this place even existed. Foreign journalists, for their part, were not to be outdone, and took great delight in spreading the most outlandish rumours as well. And then the various media outlets began rehashing each other's copy, each distorting the original story just a little more, before the whole lot was churned through the mega-blender of social media to produce a dog's dinner – as utterly fake as it was nonsensical – which had no other function but to generate clicks and retweets. A massive triumph for mediocrity.

Quite apart from the fear that the island was sheltering a potential killer, this, I think, was what was driving the Beaumont residents out of their minds. Seeing their island, their home, their lives being paraded like this under the sleazy spotlight of news à la twenty-first century. There was a profound sense of shock, nurtured by the mantra that everyone I'd come across had been repeating: nothing will ever be the same again.

Moreover, from the smallest of fishing dinghies to far more impressive vessels, everyone here owned a boat and the ban on using them felt like living under house arrest. The cops from the mainland who were patrolling the harbour were seen as invaders. This intrusion was all the harder to bear because until now the investigators didn't appear to have achieved a great deal, other than pour scorn on the people of Beaumont. They had searched the few bars and restaurants on the island, as well as a handful of shops likely to have a cold store or a large freezer, but there was nothing to suggest these inquiries had borne any fruit.

The sound of a notification on my phone prompted me to emerge from under my bedclothes. I rubbed my eyes before looking at what had come up on my screen. Laurent Lafaury had just published two articles, one straight after the other. I went onto his blog. The first post was illustrated by a photo of his swollen face. He was describing an assault he claimed he'd been subjected to the previous night, while having a drink at the bar at Yeast of Eden. A group of customers had allegedly taken him to task, rebuking him for stoking the hysteria that was beginning to take hold on the island thanks to his various tweets. Lafaury had whipped out his phone to film the scene, but according to him Ange Agostini, the local policeman, had seized his device before letting the owner of the bar give him a real thrashing, egged on by some of the others. The journalist declared he intended to press charges and ended his post by alluding to the 'scapegoat' theory popularised by René Girard: every society or community in a state of crisis will feel the need to identify and stigmatise scapegoats, so as to blame them for causing the misfortunes suffered by everyone.

In this last observation, Lafaury was clear and coherent, and he wasn't wrong. The journalist embodied the collective sense of loathing. He was living through his finest hour and the most terrible ordeal all at once. He legitimately believed he was doing his job, whereas a section of the islanders felt he was simply adding fuel to the fire. The island had keeled over into the realm of the irrational, and it wasn't hard to imagine he might fall victim to other outbursts of violence. To calm people down, and avoid things spiralling out of control, the authorities would have had to lift the blockade – something the prefecture still seemed unwilling to do. But above all, the perpetrator of this heinous crime had to be found without delay.

The journalist's second post concerned the police inquiry and, more directly, the character and backstory of the victim.

Born Apolline Mérignac in 1980, Apolline Chapuis grew up in the 7th arrondissement in Paris. She began her schooling at the École Sainte-Clotilde and went on to the Lycée

Fénelon Sainte-Marie. A shy, brilliant pupil, she gained admission to a preparatory class, specialising in the humanities, to cram for entry to a prestigious *grande école*; but in 1998, during her second year in *classe prépa*, her life veered dramatically off the rails.

At a student party, she met Karim Amrani, a small-time drug dealer who operated along Boulevard de la Chapelle, and fell madly in love. Amrani had dropped out of law school in Nanterre. He was a smooth talker, a bit of a loser and close to the far left, who would dream of being Fidel Castro one day and Tony Montana from *Scarface* the next.

To please Karim, Apolline began skipping classes and moved into a squat with him on Rue de Châteaudun. Little by little, he turned into a junkie himself. He needed more and more cash to pay for his fixes. Despite her family's best efforts to save her, Apolline was sucked into life on the margins of society. She began working as a prostitute, but soon the income from her punters was no longer enough. She then became Karim's accomplice and together they plunged head first into a world of crime.

A whole series of thefts ensued, sometimes accompanied by violence, which culminated in September 2000 with a hold-up at a bar-cum-betting shop near Place Stalingrad. The raid didn't go well. The owner put up a fight. To scare him off, Karim opened fire with a lead-shot pistol (the man would lose an eye as a result of his injury). He grabbed the cashbox and ran back outside to Apolline who was waiting on a motorbike. They were eventually spotted by a police car, triggering a high-speed chase which ended – thankfully without any casualties – on Boulevard Poissonière, just outside Le Grand Rex. When it came to the trial, Karim was sentenced to eight years in prison. Apolline got away with half of that.

Of course . . . I now remembered that some of the dates had puzzled me when I'd been scrolling through her website, as if Apolline had had a long gap in her CV.

The years drifted by. She was released from jail in Fleury-Mérogis in 2003 and put her life back on the straight and narrow. She resumed her studies in Bordeaux, then Montpellier, and married Rémi Chapuis, the son of a local lawyer whom she would divorce a few years later without having had any children. In 2012 she returned to Bordeaux, set up her wine consultancy and eventually came out, late in life – in fact, the woman who reported her disappearance to police headquarters in Bordeaux was one of her ex-partners.

At the end of his blog, Lafaury had scanned in an old cutting from *Le Parisien* reporting on the trial of the 'Bonnie and Clyde of Stalingrad'. A black and white photo showed Apolline as a tall, waif-like girl with a long face and hollow cheeks, her eyes cast down. Karim was shorter, powerful and stocky, with a forceful look about him. He had a reputation for potentially being brutal and violent when under the influence of drugs, but during the trial he'd behaved like someone who was clean. Against his lawyer's advice, he'd tried to clear Apolline's name as far as he could. A strategy that had paid off rather well.

As I finished reading the post, I found myself thinking that the revelation of Apolline Chapuis's criminal past might be just the kind of thing to calm people's nerves. Perhaps her murder had nothing to do with Beaumont, nor with its residents. Perhaps she could have been killed pretty much anywhere. I also wondered what had happened to Karim

Amrani once he'd got out of jail. Had he reverted to a life of crime? Had he tried to get in touch with his former accomplice again? Was he really the one who, at the time, had exerted such a stranglehold over Apolline, or were things more complicated? Above all, I wondered whether it was possible that, twenty years later, Apolline's murky past had come hurtling back at her like a boomerang.

I grabbed my laptop from the foot of the bed to take some notes for my novel. I'd been writing frenetically since the previous day, page after page practically typing itself. I had no idea whether what I was writing was any good, but I knew that fate had set me on the path towards a story that someone had to tell. A true story, more compelling than any work of fiction, and one which I sensed had only just begun. Why was I so convinced that Apolline's murder was merely the tip of an iceberg that was still largely under water? Maybe the feverish anxiety of the locals seemed a little suspect, as if the island were hiding a secret it wasn't prepared to reveal. In any case, I had become – once and for all – a character in a novel, like those books where you're the hero which I used to read as a child.

This feeling was to become even stronger over the next minute. My phone rang and an unknown number came up, but the area code implied it had to be someone on the island.

When I answered, I recognised Nathan Fawles's voice immediately.

He was asking me to come and see him at home.

Right away.

3.

This time Fawles didn't greet me with a volley of gunfire, but rather with a fine cup of coffee. The inside of the house was just as I'd imagined it: both minimalist and spectacular, the stark purity of stone combined with a cosy feel. The perfect home for a writer. I could easily see people like Hemingway, Neruda or Simenon writing here. Or, for that matter, Nathan Fawles . . .

He was dressed in jeans, a white shirt and a zip-neck jumper, and was busy giving his dog some water. Without his Panama hat and sunglasses, I could finally see what he really looked like. To be honest, he hadn't aged that much compared to photos from the late 1990s. Fawles was of medium build, but he commanded a real presence. His face was tanned, and his eyes were as bright as the translucent water you could see in the distance. His designer stubble and hair verged more on the pepper than the salt. Something elusive and mysterious shone from within. A force that was deep and solemn, and yet as bright as a star. A dark radiance – one you didn't know whether to trust or not.

'Come, let's sit outside,' he said, grabbing a small worn leather satchel. It was lying on an Eames chair which must have been twice my age.

I followed him onto the terrace. It was still a bit chilly, but the sun had come up. At the far left, where Fawles had been standing guard the first time I'd met him, the paving gave way to an expanse of beaten earth before the rocks reclaimed their rightful place. Anchored in the ground below three huge umbrella pines was a table with metal legs, flanked by two stone benches.

Fawles invited me to sit down and took a seat facing me.

'I'll get straight to the point,' he said, his eyes boring into mine. 'The reason I asked you here is because I need you.'

'Need me?'

'I need your help.'

'My help?'

'Stop repeating what I'm saying, it's annoying. I need you to do something. Are you with me?'

'What?'

'Something important. And risky.'

'But . . . if it's risky, what about me? What do I get in return?'

Fawles placed his satchel on the surface of the table which was covered in ceramic tiles.

'You get what's in this bag.'

'I couldn't care less what's in your bag.'

He rolled his eyes.

'Dammit, how can you say you don't care when you don't even know what's inside?'

'What I want is for you to read what I've written.'

Fawles calmly opened the satchel and took out the novel I had flung at him when we first met.

'I've read your book already, kid!' he said, smiling.

He handed me the manuscript of Crown Shyness, clearly delighted at having duped me.

I feverishly turned the pages. They were heavily annotated. Not only had Fawles read my novel, but he had also made painstaking corrections, spending considerable time doing so. I was suddenly overcome by anxiety. I'd been able to tolerate rejection from various publishers, and condescending words from an imbecile like Bernard Dufy, but would I be able to recover from sarcastic comments from my personal hero?

'What did you think?' I asked, petrified.

'Honestly?'

'Honestly. Is it crap?'

Fawles played the sadist to perfection. He took a sip of coffee, and seemed to take all the time in the world before blurting out:

'Well, to begin with, I really like the title – how it sounds, its symbolism . . .'

I could hardly breathe.

'And then I have to admit it's quite well written . . .'

I heaved a sigh of relief, even if I knew that, for Fawles, 'well written' wasn't necessarily a compliment – something which, moreover, he was quick to point out:

'I'd go as far as to say it's a little *too* well written.'

He picked up the manuscript in turn and flicked through it:

'I noticed you'd pinched two or three little writing tricks from me. And from Stephen King, Cormac McCarthy and Margaret Atwood . . .'

I didn't know if I was meant to say something in response. The sound of the waves, floating up to us from the base of the cliff, was so loud it felt like being on the deck of a boat.

'But that's no big deal,' he continued, 'it's quite normal to have people you copy when you're starting out, and at least it proves you've read some good books.'

He carried on leafing through the pages to look at his annotations again.

'You've got plot twists, the dialogue's often very well

written, sometimes it's quite funny, and you couldn't possibly say it's boring . . .'

'But?'

'But it's missing the one key thing.'

Seriously? After all that . . .

'And what's the one key thing?' I asked, feeling quite hurt.

'What do you think?'

'I don't know. Originality? New ideas?'

'Nope. Don't give a toss about ideas. They're everywhere.'

'The mechanics of the story? The balance between a good story and interesting characters?'

'Mechanics, that's for guys who fix your car. And making things balance, that's for folk who're good at math. That's not going to make you a good novelist.'

'Finding just the right word?'

'The right word is useful in a conversation,' he sneered. 'But anyone can use a dictionary. Think about it. What's *really* important?'

'What's important is readers liking your book.'

'Readers are important, true. You write for them, granted, but trying to please them is the best way of ensuring they never read you at all.'

'Well, I don't know then. What's the key thing?'

'The key thing is life. Or rather, the essence, the *sap* of life. The sap that nourishes every last bit of your story. The sap that needs to possess your whole being, racing through you, like electricity. The sap that needs to burn through your veins, so you can't help but sprint to the end of your novel, as if your very existence depended on it. That's what it means, writing. That's what'll capture your reader, pulling them in, until they've lost their bearings and they're completely, utterly submerged in your story, just as you once were yourself.'

I digested what he'd just said to me, and then plucked up the courage to ask a question:

'So basically, what's the problem with my writing?'

'It's too dry. I've no sense of urgency. But more importantly – and more seriously – I don't feel any emotions.'

'But there's plenty in there!'

Fawles shook his head.

'Fake ones. Artificial emotions, which are simply the worst . . .'

He cracked his knuckles and clarified his thinking:

'A novel's all about the emotion, not the intellect. But to create emotions, you've got to experience them in the first place. You've got to *feel* your characters' emotions. Physically. That's *all* your characters: the heroes and the scumbags too.'

'Is that it then? Is that what a novelist's real job is? Creating emotions?'

Fawles shrugged.

'At least, that's what *I* expect, when I'm reading a novel.'

'When I came asking you for advice, why did you say to me: "Do something else with your life, apart from wanting to be a writer"?'

Fawles sighed:

'Because it's no job for people in their right minds. It's a job for schizophrenics. An activity that requires destructive mental dissociation: in order to write, you've got to be in the world and outside it at the same time. Do you see what I mean?'

'Um, I think so, yes.'

'When you're writing, you're not living with your wife, or your kids, or your friends. Or rather, you pretend you're living with them. But in truth you're spending your real life with your characters, for a year, or maybe two, or even five . . .'

He was on a roll now:

'Being a novelist isn't a part-time job. If you're a novelist, you're a novelist 24/7. You never have any time off. You're always on the alert, always on the lookout for some passing thought, some expression, some personality trait that might feed into one of your characters.'

I drank in his words. It was great to hear him talking about writing with such passion. This was the Nathan Fawles I'd hoped to find by coming to the Isle of Beaumont.

'But it's still worth it, isn't it, Nathan?'

'Yes, it's worth it,' he replied, getting carried away. 'And do you know why?'

This time, yes, I had a feeling I knew:

'Because, for a short time, you're God.'

'Exactly. It sounds goddamn stupid to say it, but for a brief moment, when you're in front of your screen, you're a demiurge who can make or break people's lives. And when you've felt that euphoria, there's nothing that gives you more of a turn-on.'

The opportunity was too good to miss:

'So why stop doing it then? Why did you give up writing, Nathan?'

Fawles stopped speaking and his face hardened. The gleam faded from his eyes. Their turquoise colour had almost turned navy blue, as if an artist had just mixed in a few drops of black ink.

'Fuck . . .'

Uttered in barely a whisper, the word had practically slipped out by itself. Something had snapped.

'I stopped writing because I didn't have any strength left, that's all.'

'But you look like you're in great shape? And at the time you were only thirty-five.'

'I'm talking psychological strength. I wasn't in the right frame of mind. I didn't have the mental agility you need to write.'

'But why?'

'That's *my* problem,' he replied, putting my manuscript back in his satchel. Its lock clicked into place.

And I realised the literary masterclass was over, and we were about to move on to something else.

4.

'Right then. Are you fucking gonna help me, or what?'

Fawles looked serious. He caught my eye and stared at me unflinchingly.

'What do you want me to do?'

'Well, firstly, I'd like you to dig up some info on a woman.'

'Who?'

'A Swiss journalist who's on the island. A certain Mathilde Monney.'

'I know just who she is!' I exclaimed. 'I had no idea she was a journalist. She dropped into the shop this weekend. She even bought all your books!'

The news left Fawles unmoved.

'What do you want to know about her, exactly?'

'Whatever you can find out: why she's here, what she does during the day, who she meets, what sort of questions she's asking people.'

'Do you think she's looking to write an article about you?'

Once again, Fawles ignored my question.

'Next, I want you to go to her place and get yourself into her room.'

'And do what to her?'

'Zilch, you moron! You get into her room when she's not there.'

'Um, that's against the law, you know—'

'If you only want to do what's legal, you'll never be a good novelist. And you'll never be an artist. The history of art is the history of breaking the rules.'

'You're playing with words there, Nathan.'

'It's what writers do.'

'I thought you'd stopped being a writer.'

'Once a writer, always a writer.'

'Bit lame as a citation for a Pulitzer Prize, isn't it?'

'Shut up.'

'OK, so what am I supposed to find in this room?'

'I don't really know. Photos, some articles, stuff on computers or something . . .'

He poured himself another cup of coffee and winced as he swallowed a mouthful.

'And then, I want you to trawl the internet for anything you can find on Mathilde, and then . . .'

I'd already whipped out my phone to begin my research, but Fawles stopped me.

'Just listen, will you! And don't waste your time: there's no Wi-Fi or networks here.'

I put my device away like a pupil who's been caught red-handed.

'I also want you to research two names: Apolline Chapuis and—'

My jaw dropped. I butted in:

'The woman who was murdered?'

Fawles knitted his brow.

'What the heck are you on about?'

From the look on his face, I realised the writer lived such a solitary life that news of the terrible events that had shaken Beaumont for several days – and the circumstances surrounding them – hadn't yet filtered through to him. I brought him up to speed with everything I knew: Apolline's murder, her frozen body, her criminal past as Karim's accomplice, the blockade of the island.

As I rattled through the facts, I could see his astonishment steadily growing, seeping into his eyes and across his face. The initial anxiety I'd detected on arriving at his home had given way to total alarm, and a palpable sense of fear which now occupied his entire being.

When I'd finished speaking, Fawles looked dazed. He needed a moment to gather himself, but finally regained his composure. And, after a moment's hesitation, he confided in me in turn, by sharing the story Mathilde Monney had told him the day before – the tale of Apolline and Karim losing their camera, and its incredible journey. At that precise moment I was struggling to understand it all. I was faced with such a deluge of information that I simply couldn't piece everything together. I had plenty of questions for Fawles, but he didn't give me any time. Barely had he wrapped up his story than he grabbed me by the arm and saw me to the door.

'Get a move on! I want you searching Mathilde's room *right now!*'

'I can't go right now. I've got to get back to work, at the shop.'

'For God's sake boy, sort your shit out!' he yelled. 'Just get on the damn case, will you!'

He slammed the door on me. I suddenly realised how serious the whole thing was, and that I had better do what Fawles had asked.

7

HIGH NOON

1.

Western tip of the island

Mathilde Monney slammed the door of her pickup, switched on the engine and made a U-turn on the gravel road. From the outside, the guest house where the journalist was staying looked like an English cottage. A little half-timbered house with a thatched roof whose facade, clad in marbled stone, had been colonised by climbing roses. Behind it stretched a wild garden, which extended as far as an old double-arched bridge giving access to the Sainte-Sophie peninsula.

I had only been to the west coast twice. The first time to take a look at the nearby convent where the Benedictine nuns lived, and the second with Ange Agostini, the day Apolline's body had been discovered close to Tristana Beach. When I'd first landed on the island, Audibert had explained that, historically, this part of Beaumont was the favoured haunt of the Anglophone community. And, as it happened,

Mathilde was lodging with an old Irish woman. For many years now the cottage had belonged to Colleen Dunbar, a former architect who topped up her income by renting out an upstairs room on a bed and breakfast basis.

In order to get here, I'd abandoned my bike – I'd had a puncture while coming back from Fawles's house – and hired an electric scooter outside Ed's Corner which I'd hidden away in a thicket. I'd had to negotiate hard with Audibert to get the morning off. The bookseller was becoming more and more prickly, as if he were carrying all the woes of the world on his shoulders.

While waiting for the coast to clear, I'd made my way down the rocks at a spot where the drop was less steep. From my lookout post, I drank in the stunning beauty of this rugged corner of the island while keeping the cottage in my sights. Twenty minutes earlier, I'd caught sight of the old Dunbar woman as she left the house. Her daughter had come to pick her up in the car to take her shopping. Mathilde was preparing to leave too. Her vehicle pulled away from the property and turned towards the east, where there was a straight, flat stretch of road. I waited until she'd disappeared from view before leaving my hideout, climbing back up the rocks and heading towards the cottage.

A quick glance around reassured me. There were no neighbours close by. The convent must have been more than a hundred metres away. If I focused really hard, I could just make out two or three nuns busy at work in their kitchen garden, but as soon as I slipped around the back of the house, they couldn't see me any longer.

To be honest, I wasn't terribly comfortable with the idea of doing something illegal. All my life I'd been a willing victim of *good student syndrome*. I was an only child, born of those middle classes who could barely manage to make ends meet. My parents had always invested a great deal – their time, their energy, the little money they did earn – so that I'd do well in my studies and become a 'good person'. From a young age, I'd tried my hardest not to disappoint them and to avoid screwing things up. And that Boy Scout side of my nature had become ingrained. My adolescence had been a long, quiet river. I'd maybe smoked three cigarettes in the playground when I was fourteen, jumped the lights two or three times on my scooter, recorded a few pornos from Canal+ and beaten up a guy in revenge for a nasty tackle at football, but that was more or less it.

My student years were marked by the same dead calm. I'd got hammered twice, 'borrowed' a snakewood fountain pen that belonged to another student at my business school, and stolen a classy Pléiade edition of Georges Simenon from L'Œil Écoute, a bookshop on Boulevard du Montparnasse. Since then, the shop had gone out of business, and each time I went past the clothing store which had replaced it I wondered whether I'd played some part in them going under.

On a more serious note, I'd never smoked a single joint nor touched drugs of any kind – truth be told, I wouldn't even have known how to get hold of them. I wasn't a party animal, I needed my eight hours of sleep a night, and for two years I'd been working flat out every day, including weekends and holidays, either writing my book or doing the mundane jobs that paid the rent. Had I been in a novel, I could have played to perfection the role of the naive, sentimental young man who'll end up callous and hard, thanks to the investigation and all its twists and turns.

So I tried to look casual and relaxed as I walked towards the front door. Everyone had sworn to me that people on Beaumont never locked their doors. I tried turning the handle, which remained hopelessly wedged in place. Yet another of those tales the islanders had apparently been trotting out to visitors, or poor gullible souls like me. Or perhaps the discovery of Apolline's body just a few kilometres from here had prompted the journalist to be more cautious.

I would have to force my way in. I examined the glazed kitchen door, but the glass seemed too thick for me to break it easily without hurting myself. I returned to the back of the house. In the distance, the nuns appeared to have deserted the kitchen garden. I tried to remain positive. I simply had to find a pane that wasn't as tough, and smash it using my elbow. On the terrace – evidently constructed in a rush – the Irish woman had set up a shoddy-looking table in greyish teak and three chairs which the sun, rain and salty sea air had completely worn away. And here, behind this little patio, I was pleasantly surprised to see that one side of the French windows had been left open. Too good to be true?

2.

I entered the living room. It was calm and overheated. The warm, sickly-sweet aroma of apple and cinnamon tart hovered in the air. The decor was pleasant and inviting: a chocolate box with a very British flavour, featuring a host of candles, tartan rugs, curtains in flowery patterns, romantic fabrics and ornamental plates hung on the walls.

I was about to go upstairs when I heard a sound. I swirled around to find a Great Dane bearing down on me. He stopped less than a metre away, poised to attack. He was one enormous ball of muscle, with dark, glistening fur, who came up to my navel. His ears were pricked and he was staring at me with hostile eyes, growling. I was terrified. Around his neck he was wearing a sort of large medallion, engraved with the words 'Little Max'. A name that probably sounded cute when he was only two or three months old, but no longer seemed very appropriate. I quickly tried to back off, but that didn't stop the dog charging straight at me. I dodged aside just in time and dashed onto the staircase, sensing the hound at my heels, about to sink his fangs into my leg as I raced up. With one last effort, I propelled myself to the top of the stairs, shot into the first room I came to and flung the door shut behind me, literally slamming it in the dog's face.

While he hurled himself at the door, barking furiously, I caught my breath and pulled myself together. By a stroke of luck – well, in a manner of speaking, as I'd only narrowly avoided losing one of my feet – I was obviously in the very room currently occupied by Mathilde.

It was a studio of some kind, with exposed beams in pale wood, haunted by the ghost of Laura Ashley. Bouquets of dried flowers were arranged on weathered pieces of furniture, repainted in pastel tones, while the curtains and bedspread were adorned with idyllic pastoral and bucolic motifs. But Mathilde had reconfigured her guest bedroom into a bizarre sort of operations centre. The perfect war room, in fact, dedicated to a single obsession: Nathan Fawles.

A squat vintage armchair in pink velvet was groaning

under the weight of books and files. The big table had been turned into a desk, and a pretty dressing table with a mirror had become a stand for her printer. While Little Max steadily worked himself into a frenzy outside the door, I began looking through all the documents.

It was obvious that Mathilde Monney was conducting a full-blown investigation into Fawles. There was no laptop on her workspace, but there were dozens of articles printed out and marked with a highlighter. I knew what they were. They were the ones that invariably popped up whenever you searched online: the same old interviews from the 1990s, carried out before Fawles had stopped writing, and then those two key articles, the one from the *New York Times* in 2010, 'The Invisible Man', and the one from the US edition of *Vanity Fair* three years earlier, 'Fawles or False? (and Vice Versa)'.

Mathilde had also annotated the writer's three books and printed out numerous photos of Nathan. In particular, screenshots from the last time he'd been a guest on Bernard Pivot's programme, *Bouillon de culture*. For some reason that escaped me, the journalist had zoomed in on . . . the shoes Fawles had been wearing during the show. I examined her papers more closely. By logging on to special-interest forums, Mathilde thought she'd identified the exact style: elasticated Weston 'Le Cambre 705' ankle boots in brown calfskin.

I scratched my head. What was the point of all this? The journalist clearly wasn't writing one of those endless seasonal features on the Isle of Beaumont's recluse. Her investigation into Fawles bore all the hallmarks of a police inquiry. But what could her motive be?

As I delved into the hardback files stacked high on the arm-chair, I made another discovery: some photos, taken with a telephoto lens, of a man whom you saw in a series of different locations. A North African, a good forty or so years old, in a T-shirt and denim jacket. I recognised the setting immediately: Essonne, and more specifically the town of Évry. There was no mistaking it. There were more than enough pictures of the area. The cathedral with its contentious architecture, the Évry 2 shopping centre, the Parc des Coquibus, the esplanade outside Évry-Courcouronnes station.

In my final year at business school, I'd had a girlfriend who lived there. Joanna Pawlowski. Third runner-up in the Miss Île-de-France competition 2014. The prettiest face you could imagine. Huge green eyes, those lovely blonde features, so typically Polish, a gentleness and grace in her every movement. I would often see her home after classes. During our never-ending journey – the RER D train from the Gare du Nord to Évry – I would try to convert her to my faith, whose central doctrine was reading. I had presented her with my favourite books – *The Unfinished Romance*, *The Horseman on the Roof*, *Her Lover* – but nothing had worked. Joanna had the look of a romantic heroine, yet she was anything but romantic. I had my head in the clouds; she was utterly down to earth. She was firmly entrenched in the real and the physical, whereas my world was centred on emotions.

She left me at the same time as she dropped out of university to work in a jeweller's in a shopping mall. Six months later, she summoned me to a café to break the news that she was marrying Jean-Pascal Péchard, known as JPP, one of the department heads at the hypermarket in the same shopping centre. The poems I'd carried on writing for her had paled in comparison to the house in Savigny-sur-Orge that JPP had bought by taking out a mortgage for twenty-five years. To soothe my wounded pride, I'd told myself that, one day, she'd regret it, when she heard me discussing my first novel on TV, on the literary talk show *La Grande Librairie*. In the meantime, I was left feeling down for a long time. Whenever I thought about Joanna, or looked at a photo of her on my phone, it took me a long while to admit that the delicate nature of her features was no indication of a delicate mind. And why would the two be connected anyway? It was one of those fallacies I had to drum into my head to avoid further disappointment.

The sound of the dog barking outside the door roused me from my thoughts, and reminded me of the urgency of the situation. I plunged back into the photos. They were date-stamped 12 August 2018. Who had taken them? A cop, a private detective, Mathilde herself? And more importantly, who was this man? Suddenly, thanks to a pose where you could see his face more clearly, the penny dropped: it was Karim Amrani. Twenty years older and weighing as many kilos more.

After his stay in prison, the former little thug from Boulevard de la Chapelle had apparently gone to live in Essonne. In other shots, you could see him chatting with mechanics, or entering and leaving a garage where he seemed to be the manager or the owner. Had he gone straight too, just like Apolline? And was his life, in turn, now in danger as well? I had neither the time nor the information I needed to answer these questions. I wasn't sure whether to take any of these items. I finally decided to take photos of the most important ones with my phone, so as to leave no trace of my visit.

The questions continued to swirl around in my head. Why was Mathilde interested in Amrani? No doubt because of this business with the camera, but what was the link with Fawles? In the hope of finding out, I decided to conduct a more thorough search of both bedroom and bathroom before leaving. Nothing under the mattress, nor in the drawers or cupboards. I lifted the lid of the cistern to examine the inside and tested the wooden floor with my foot. It felt a bit rickety in some places, but I couldn't find any removable boards that might have concealed a hiding place.

Behind the toilet, on the other hand, one of the skirting boards popped out as soon as I touched it. Without holding out much hope, I crouched down and slipped my forearm into the gap, only to find a thick bundle of letters held together with an elastic band. Just as I was about to look at them in more detail, I heard the sound of an engine. Little Max stopped barking his head off at the door and bolted down the stairs. I took a peek between the curtains. Colleen Dunbar and her daughter were back already. I hastily folded the bundle of letters and stuffed it down the inside pocket of my jacket. I waited until the two women had disappeared from my field of vision before lifting the sash window which looked onto the roof of a shed. From there, I jumped down onto the lawn and, with my legs wobbling like jelly, I sprinted across the road to retrieve my scooter.

As I was trying to get the thing started, I heard barking behind me. The Great Dane was in pursuit, and hurtling in my direction. The moped crawled along the first few metres, barely managing forty kilometres an hour, but luckily gathered speed thanks to a perfectly timed slope – which gave me the chance to stick a finger up at the dog as he finally gave in, limping back home with his tail between his legs.

Fuck you, Little Max . . .

3.

The sun was hot and high in the sky, as if it were summer again. The wind had warmed up and quietened down a little. Wearing canvas shorts and a Blondie T-shirt, Mathilde skipped from rock to rock with ease.

Pine Cove was one of the most breathtaking spots on the island. A little inlet, deep and narrow, gouged from rock of dazzling whiteness.

Getting there required determination, and quite a bit of effort. Mathilde had left her pickup in the parking area overlooking Les Ondes Beach, and then followed a path hollowed into the granite like a maze. It had taken her a good hour's walk to reach the cove. Starting off with a deceptively flat stretch, the track became steeper as it climbed a rugged, craggy slope which offered panoramic views, both wild and spectacular in equal measure.

Then the path wound down towards the beach, a heart-stoppingly perilous descent. The last few metres were the hardest as they plunged so sharply, but it was a risk well worth taking. When you arrived on the beach, it felt as though you were at the very ends of the earth, in some lost paradise: turquoise water, ochre sand, the cooling shade of pines and the heady scent of eucalyptus. There were even some caves not far away, but it was forbidden to reveal their existence to tourists.

Shaped like a half-moon, and sheltered from the wind by granite cliffs, the beach was relatively small. During the months of July and August you could sometimes feel hemmed in because of the crowds, but on this October morning the place lay completely deserted. About fifty metres away, facing the cove, a tiny islet rose from the sea: a needle of rock soaring into the sky which bore the name Punta dell'Ago. In the summer, reckless teenagers would get their kicks by scrambling up barefoot and diving into the water. One of the island's rites of passage.

Mathilde stared at the horizon from behind her sunglasses. Fawles had anchored his boat beside the rocky outcrop. The Riva's chrome fittings and glossy mahogany hull gleamed in the afternoon sun. You could almost have believed you were in Italy, back in the days of *la dolce vita*, or a little bay in the Saint-Tropez of the sixties.

She waved to him from a distance, but he didn't seem willing to come any closer to let her jump on board.

If the mountain won't come to Muhammad . . .

After all, she did have her swimsuit on. She pulled off her shorts and T-shirt and put them in her bag which she wedged at the base of some rocks, taking only her phone in its protective waterproof case.

The water was cold, but crystal clear. She waded two or three metres into the sea and then dived in without thinking twice. A freezing wave swept over her, but the cold quickly wore off as she began swimming. The young woman had the Riva in her line of sight. Fawles was standing at the wheel, dressed in a navy-blue polo shirt and light-coloured trousers. He watched her come closer with his arms folded. His face, hidden by sunglasses, remained inscrutable. When Mathilde was only a few strokes away, he held out his hand, yet appeared to hesitate for a couple of seconds before eventually helping her to drag herself onto the boat.

'For a moment there, I thought you were going to try and drown me.'

'Perhaps I should have,' he said, handing her a towel.

She moved across to sit on the banquette, upholstered in turquoise-blue leather – the famous Aquamarine blue from the Pantone range which gave the boat its name.

'Charming!' she exclaimed, rubbing her hair, neck and arms.

Fawles came over to her.

'It really wasn't the smartest idea, meeting like this. I had to get my boat out, even with the blockade on.'

Mathilde spread her hands helplessly.

'Well, you're here now, which means you're keen to hear more! The truth always comes at a price.'

Fawles was in a foul mood.

'So you think it's funny, do you?' he asked.

'Listen, do you want the rest of the story or not?'

'If you think I'm going to beg for it, you're wrong. You're more desperate to tell me what happened than I am to hear it.'

'Fine. Whatever.'

She made as if to dive in again, but he held her back by the arm.

'Oh, for God's sake, grow up! Come on then, what was in those photos on the camera?'

Mathilde grabbed the strap of the waterproof case which she'd placed on the seat. She turned on her phone, opened the Photo app and increased the brightness as far as it would go before showing Fawles the pictures she'd chosen.

'Those are the last shots that were taken, dated July 2000.'

Fawles flicked through them by swiping the screen. They were precisely what he expected. Holiday snaps, taken in Hawaii by the partners-in-crime who'd lost the camera: Apolline and Karim heading to the beach, Apolline and Karim having a shag, Apolline and Karim getting plastered, Apolline and Karim going scuba diving.

The other images Mathilde showed him were older; they had been taken a month earlier. Fawles scrolled through and was suddenly caught off guard. The photos rammed into him, like a punch in the gut. They showed a family of three celebrating a birthday. A man, a woman and their son who was about ten. It was spring and they'd had dinner on the terrace. Night was about to fall, but the sky was still pink. Behind them, you could make out some trees and the familiar Paris skyline, and even the silhouette of the Eiffel Tower.

'Take a good look at the little boy,' said Mathilde in a strained voice as she picked out a close-up shot.

Shading the screen from the sun, Fawles studied the child closely. An impish little face, eyes that sparkled behind a pair of red-rimmed glasses, a mop of tousled blond hair, the French flag daubed across his cheeks. He was wearing the French football team's blue jersey and making the V for victory sign with his fingers. He looked sweet and kind – and a tad mischievous too.

'Do you know his name?' she asked.

Fawles shook his head.

'He was called Théo,' she said. 'Théo Verneuil. He was celebrating his eleventh birthday that evening. It was Sunday 11 June 2000, the night of the French team's first match in the Euros.'

'Why are you showing me this?'

'Do you know what happened to him? About three hours after this photo was taken, that same night, Théo was killed by a bullet in his back.'

4.

Fawles didn't bat an eyelid. His eyes swept across the screen, examining the photos of the child's parents more intently. The father, a handsome forty-something, with keen eyes, a tanned complexion and a determined jaw, embodied a certain self-confidence, the urge to take action and forge ahead in life. The mother, a pretty woman with a stylish chignon, remained more in the background.

'Do you know who they are?' asked Mathilde.

'Yes, it's the Verneuil family. They talked enough about this business at the time for me to remember.'

'And what do you remember, exactly?'

Fawles narrowed his eyes, and massaged his stubble with the flat of his hand.

'Alexandre Verneuil was involved in philanthropic medicine, and politically close to the left. He was part of the second wave of "French doctors", a movement committed to charitable work overseas. He had written a few books, and sometimes appeared in the media to talk about bioethics or humanitarian intervention. As I recall, it was just when he was really starting to get recognised by the public that he was murdered at home, along with his wife and son.'

'His wife was called Sofia,' said Mathilde.

'I don't remember that,' he said, edging away from the banquette. 'But I do remember clearly that it was the circumstances surrounding these murders that shocked people, more than anything else. The killer – or killers, perhaps – broke into the Verneuils' apartment and slaughtered the entire family, and the investigation was never able to establish a motive for the massacre, nor the identity of the culprit, or culprits.'

'Well, as for the motive, they always thought it was burglary,' said Mathilde, moving towards the prow of the boat. 'Some valuable watches and jewellery went missing, along with . . . along with a camera.'

Fawles was beginning to see the light.

'Ah, so that's your theory: you think you've found the people who murdered the Verneuil family, thanks to these photos? You think Chapuis and Amrani killed the Verneuils just to steal some stuff? They shot a kid for a few trinkets?'

'It makes sense, doesn't it? There was another burglary in the building that same night, on the floor above. The second one may simply have gone wrong.'

Fawles was getting annoyed.

'We're not reopening the case today, are we?'

'Why not? Back then, Apolline and Karim carried out a whole load of burglaries. He was high as a kite. They needed cash all the time.'

'He doesn't look that stoned to me, in the Hawaii photos.'

'How did they get hold of the camera then, if they didn't steal it?'

'Listen, I don't give a toss about this business and I don't see what it's got to do with me.'

'They found Apolline nailed to a tree a stone's throw from here! Can't you see the Verneuil affair's blowing up all over again, right here, on the island?'

'What do you want me to do about it?'

'I want you to write the end of the story.'

Fawles gave vent to his exasperation.

'What for? Go on then, tell me. Do you get off on this stuff, raking up this old case? Just because some country bumpkin in Alabama emails you some old photos, you suddenly feel vested with a mission?'

'Absolutely! Because I love people!'

He mimicked her, exaggerating for effect:

'"I *luh-ve* people." Bullshit! Can't you hear yourself talking?'

Mathilde fought back:

'What I mean is, I'm not insensitive to the fate of my fellow human beings.'

Fawles began striding back and forth on the boat.

'Well, in that case, you'd better write some pieces to alert your "fellow human beings" to climate change, the depletion of the oceans, the mass extinction of wildlife, the degradation of our biodiversity. Warn them about the plague of fake news. Put things back in context, add some distance, some perspective. Write about topics like schools and state hospitals stretched to breaking point, about the imperialism of the big multinationals, the current state of prisons and—'

'OK, Fawles, I get the idea. Thanks for the journalism lesson.'

'Basically, focus on useful stuff!'

134

'Doing justice to the dead is useful.'

He stopped abruptly and wagged his finger at her.

'The dead are dead. And where they've gone, they frankly don't give a fuck about your little articles, trust me. As for me, I'll NEVER write a single word about this business. Nor any other, for that matter.'

Infuriated, Fawles stormed off to sit in the cockpit. Facing the CinemaScope windscreen, he sank into contemplation of the distant horizon, as if he too yearned to be thousands of kilometres from where he was now.

Mathilde rode back into battle by shoving her phone under his nose, with the photo of Théo Verneuil on the screen.

'So you don't care about tracking down whoever murdered three people, including a kid?'

'Yep, cos I'm not a cop! You really want to revisit an inquiry that's almost twenty years old? For the sake of what, exactly? You're not a judge, as far as I know?'

He pretended to smack his forehead with the palm of his hand.

'Ah, yes, I'd forgotten, you're a journalist! That's even worse!'

Mathilde ignored this attack.

'I want you to help me untangle the threads of this story.'

'I hate your despicable methods and everything you stand for. I was sitting there helpless, and you went off and snatched my dog, just to make contact with me. You'll pay for this. I loathe folk like you.'

'I think I'd figured that out. And will you stop harping on about that dog! I'm talking about a child. If this kid were yours, you'd want to know who'd killed him.'

'Daft kind of logic. I don't have any kids.'

'No, obviously you don't, you don't like anyone! Correction: you *do* like your characters, your little people made of paper. The ones that come straight out of your head. They're a whole lot easier to deal with.'

She smacked her forehead.

'Oh, but no! Not even them! Because His Excellency the Esteemed Author has decided to give up writing. Not even a shopping list, is that right?'

'Get the hell out, you stupid little woman. Go on, piss off!'

Mathilde refused to move an inch.

'We're doing different jobs, Fawles. Mine's about exposing the truth. You don't know what I'm like. I'll get there. I'll get to the bottom of this.'

'Do whatever you want, I don't give a shit, but don't you ever come snooping round my house again.'

She wagged her finger ominously at him in turn:

'Oh, I'll certainly be back, I give you my word. I'll be back, and next time you'll be *forced* to help me write the end of this story. Forced to confront . . . what did you call it again? Oh yes, your *unspeakable truth*.'

This time, Fawles exploded and leapt towards Mathilde. The boat suddenly keeled to one side and the young woman let out a cry. Summoning all the strength he could find, Fawles scooped her up and sent her flying into the sea, along with her phone.

Boiling with rage, he switched on the Riva's engine and headed for The Southern Cross.

136

8

EACH PERSON IS A SHADOW

1.

After my eventful trip to Colleen Dunbar's cottage – which had concluded with my triumphant head-to-head with Little Max – I had returned to the town, where I'd sought refuge at a table at Yeast of Eden. I'd avoided the busy terrace and instead retreated inside, near a window looking onto the sea. Over a hot chocolate, I'd read and reread the letters hidden in Mathilde's room. They were all penned by the same hand, and my heart had leapt when I'd recognised the fine, sloping handwriting that belonged to Nathan Fawles. I'd had no doubt whatsoever, as I'd been online and seen several scanned manuscripts of the novels he'd donated to the New York Public Library.

There were twenty or so love letters in French, missing their envelopes, sent from Paris or New York. Only a few were dated, covering a period that stretched from April to December 1998. They were signed 'Nathan' and addressed to a mysterious woman with an unknown name. Most of them began with 'My darling', but on one of them Fawles used the letter 'S' as the initial letter of her name.

I'd paused a number of times as I was reading. Could I really get away with going through these letters and thereby delving into Fawles's private world without permission? Every last part of me was screaming no, I didn't have the right to do so. But this ethical dilemma had soon crumbled away, faced with my curiosity and a sense that I was reading documents that were as unique as they were fascinating.

Both literary and sentimental, this correspondence painted the portrait of a man who was madly in love and that of a sensitive woman, someone who glowed from within, bursting with life. It was obvious that, at the time, Fawles and this woman had been constrained to live apart, but my reading told me nothing about the obstacles that prevented the lovers from seeing each other more often.

Considered as a whole, the letters made up a hybrid work of art, a mixture of classic epistolary exchanges, poetry and stories illustrated with exquisite little watercolours painted in various shades of ochre. They weren't really a conversation. Not the kind of letters in which you told each other about your day, or what you'd had for your last meal. They were a sort of hymn to life and the fundamental need to love, despite the pain of absence, the insanity of the world – and war. The theme of war permeated all of the writing: struggle, rifts, oppression, but it wasn't easy to tell whether Fawles was referring to some ongoing armed conflict or simply using an extended metaphor.

In terms of style, the writing was studded with flashes of brilliance, daring figures of speech and biblical allusions. It revealed a new side to Fawles's talent. Its musicality reminded me of Aragon and some of his poems to his wife and muse,

Elsa Triolet, or Apollinaire's 'If I died up there . . .' from his *Poems to Lou*. The intensity of certain passages made me think of Guilleragues's *The Letters of a Portuguese Nun*. Their formal perfection even made me wonder whether these letters weren't a pure literary exercise. Had this S. existed at all, or was she nothing more than a symbol? The embodiment of the object of someone's desire. Something universal which spoke to all those in love.

A second reading had dispelled this impression. No: every word of this bled sincerity and intimacy, every line was feverish with desire, brimming with hope and plans for the future. Even if this fire and passion were also overshadowed by potential danger, lurking between certain lines.

On the third reading, I came up with yet another hypothesis: S. was ill. The war in question was the kind a woman might wage against illness. But nature, and elements related to the weather, also played a key role in the letters. The landscapes described were rich in contrast, both precise and poetic at the same time. Fawles was associated with the sun and light of the South, or the metallic skies of New York. S. was connected to something that felt more sorrowful. Mountains, a leaden sky, freezing temperatures, a 'premature darkness descending on the land of wolves'.

I checked the time on my phone. I'd arranged the morning off with Audibert, but I was supposed to be back at work at 2 p.m. I skimmed through the letters one last time, in chronological order, and a question arose in my mind: had there been more letters, or had something happened to bring this mutual attraction – physical and intellectual – to an abrupt end? Above all, I wondered what kind of woman could have aroused such passionate feelings in Fawles. I'd read just about everything written about him, but, even back when Fawles had still been speaking to the media, he'd never given away much about his private life. A thought suddenly occurred to me: what if Fawles were gay? And what if S. – the *angel with golden hair* described in the letters – were a man? Hmm, no, this theory didn't stack up, given the number of grammatical agreements which in French reflected the female sex.

My phone vibrated and a little box flashed up on the screen, indicating a series of tweets from Lafaury. He was dishing out some new information passed on from his sources. Having made the link between Apolline and Karim, the investigators had focused their inquiries on the Essonne area, looking to question the former dealer. Some cops from Évry Serious Crime had turned up at his address, in the Les Épinettes district. Not only was he not there, but his neighbours assured the officers they hadn't heard from him for almost two months now. Nor had the employees at his garage, but as none of them was especially fond of the police, no one had reported his disappearance. Lafaury's latest tweet revealed that, during a search, numerous traces of blood had been found in Karim's home. Tests were being carried out.

I made a mental note of these disturbing facts and returned to Fawles's letters. I tucked them carefully into the pocket of my jacket before getting up to go back to the shop. Breaking into Mathilde Monney's room had certainly been productive. I now held in my possession details of Fawles's life of which only I and very few others were aware. The news of these quite extraordinary letters written by a legendary author would, without a shadow of a doubt, drop like a bombshell in the publishing world. At the end of the 1990s, shortly before announcing his definitive exit from the literary stage, Nathan Fawles had been passionately in love – a passion that had swept him away and consumed everything in his path. But something unknown, some catastrophic event, had ended this relationship and broken the writer's heart. Since then, Fawles had placed his life on hold and given up writing – and no doubt sealed off his heart for ever too.

Everything suggested that this woman, the *angel with golden hair*, was the key to unlocking Fawles's secret. The hidden face of his darkness.

His 'rosebud'.

Had Fawles asked me to investigate Mathilde in order to retrieve these letters and ensure his secret remained safe? How had the journalist managed to get hold of this correspondence? And, more importantly, why had she stashed it behind a skirting board, the way you'd hide cash or drugs?

2.

'Nathan! Nathan! Wake up!'

It was 9 p.m. and pitch black at The Southern Cross. Having rung for ten minutes without getting an answer, I'd decided to climb over the outer wall. I'd practically fumbled my way through the dark, not daring to switch on the torch in my phone. My heart was in my mouth. I thought the golden retriever was going to pounce on me, and I'd already had my fill of dogs for the day – but good old Bronco had instead welcomed me like a saviour, leading me to his master who was lying on the terrace. The writer had collapsed onto the stone paving, and was now curled up in foetal position, an empty bottle of whisky by his side.

Fawles was patently smashed out of his skull.

'Nathan! Nathan!' I shouted as I shook him.

I turned on all the external lights. Then I returned to sit beside him. His breathing was heavy and erratic. I gradually managed to make him come round, ably assisted by Bronco drooling over his face.

Fawles eventually got back on his feet.

'Are you OK?'

'I'm fine,' he assured me, wiping his face with his forearm. 'What the hell are you doing here?'

'I've got some news for you.'

He rubbed his temples and his eyes.

'Fucking migraine.'

I picked up the empty bottle.

'Not surprised, after what you've been knocking back.'

It was Bara No Niwa, a legendary Japanese whisky brand which appeared in all of Fawles's novels. The company had stopped production in the 1980s. Since then, the scarcity of the few remaining bottles had inflated their price to stratospheric levels. What a waste, getting drunk on something as divine as that!

'Tell me what you found at the journalist's place.'

'You'd better go and have a shower first.'

He opened his mouth to tell me to fuck off, but reason got the better of him.

'You might not be wrong.'

While he was in the bathroom I took the opportunity to explore the living room. I still couldn't get over the fact that I'd made my way into Fawles's private world. It felt as though everything connected to him had a solemn aspect to it. Positioned somewhere between Ali Baba's cavern and Plato's cave, The Southern Cross, for me, possessed an impenetrable, mysterious aura.

The first time I'd been here, I'd been struck by the absence of photos, souvenirs, all those bits and pieces that anchor a place in the past. The house wasn't cold – far from it – but it was a little impersonal. There was just one playful touch: a scale model of a sports car. A silver-grey Porsche 911 with blue and red stripes. I'd read in an American paper that Fawles had owned an identical car in the 1990s. A one-off, which the German manufacturer had made to order in 1975 for the conductor Herbert von Karajan.

Having looked round the living room, I ventured into the kitchen and opened the fridge and cupboards. I made some tea, an omelette, some toast and a green salad. I tried checking my phone at the same time, looking for news on the investigation, but the network signal was hopelessly weak.

On the worktop, beside the hob, I spotted an old-fashioned transistor radio, the kind my grandfather used to have. When I switched it on, it was tuned to classical music, so I turned the plastic dial to try to pick up a news station. Unfortunately, I only caught the tail end of the 9 p.m. bulletin on RTL. I was busy struggling to find France Info when Fawles came in.

He had changed into a white shirt and jeans, and was wearing little horn-rimmed glasses. He looked ten years younger and appeared as relaxed as if he'd just slept for eight hours.

'At your age, you really ought to go easy on the drink.'

'Shut up.'

However, he nodded to thank me for making dinner. He

took out two plates and cutlery which he laid facing each other on the counter.

'And now, some breaking news in the Isle of Beaumont murder inquiry . . .' said a voice on the radio.

We edged closer to listen in. In fact, there were two pieces of news. And the first came as a real shock. Thanks to an anonymous tip-off, Évry Serious Crime had just discovered Karim Amrani's body somewhere in Sénart Forest, not far from Évry itself. The body's advanced state of decomposition suggested he had died quite some time earlier. Apolline Chapuis's murder was suddenly turning into a much more complex affair. But from the media's point of view, paradoxically, it was about to lose its distinctiveness, becoming merely part of a far broader and far less exotic canvas – the world of organised crime, the sprawling Paris suburbs and their housing estates, and all the rest. With its focus shifting in this way, and moving elsewhere, the Isle of Beaumont case was changing into – at least, for the time being – the Amrani case instead.

The second news update went something like this: the maritime prefect had just decided – at long last – to lift the blockade around the island. A ruling which, according to France Info, would take effect from 7 a.m. the following morning. Fawles didn't seem to be particularly affected by this latest development. The crisis that had plunged him into a drunken stupor had passed. He ate his share of the omelette while recounting his conversation with Mathilde that afternoon. I was riveted by what he told me. I was too young to have any memory of the Verneuil case, but I had the feeling I'd already heard about it in one of those radio or TV programmes that revisited high-profile human interest stories. Selfishly speaking, I could see terrific potential here for a novel, but I couldn't work out what might have shaken Fawles to such an extent.

'Is that what got you into that state?'

'What state would that be?'

'The state you were in after getting pissed on whisky all afternoon.'

'Listen, stop going on about stuff that's way beyond you. I'd rather you told me what you dug up at Mathilde Monney's place.'

3.

Wisely, I chose to start by telling him about the investigation Mathilde seemed to be conducting, firstly into Karim Amrani and then into Fawles himself. When I brought up the business of the shoes, he looked completely gobsmacked.

'That girl's off her head . . . Is that all you found?'

'No, but I'm afraid you're not going to like the next bit.'

I'd piqued his curiosity, but that gave me no pleasure at all as I knew just how upset he was about to be.

'Mathilde Monney had some letters.'

'What letters?'

'Letters you wrote.'

'I've never written her a single word!'

'No, Nathan. Letters you wrote to another woman twenty years ago.'

I extracted the bundle of letters from my jacket pocket and placed them in front of him, beside the plates.

To begin with, he stared at the sheets of paper without

being able to fully comprehend they were real. He needed some time before he dared to unfold them. And then even longer before starting to read the first lines. He looked utterly morose. It was more than astonishment. It genuinely felt as though Fawles had just seen a ghost appear. Bit by bit, he managed to contain his sense of shock and regain a modicum of composure.

'Have you read them?'

'Yes I have, sorry. And I don't regret it. They're sublime. In fact, they're so perfect you ought to let someone publish them.'

'I think you'd better go, Raphaël. Thanks for everything you've done.'

His voice sounded as if it came from beyond the grave. He got up to see me out, but didn't even get as far as the door, and sent me away with a vague flick of his hand. From the doorstep, I watched him lumber over to the bar and pour himself another glass of whisky before going to sit down in his armchair. Then his eyes misted over and his mind drifted elsewhere, into the labyrinthine maquis of the past and the pain of his memories. I couldn't let that happen.

'Wait, Nathan. You've drunk enough for tonight!' I said, retracing my steps.

I planted myself in front of him and took away his glass.

'Just fucking leave me alone!'

'Try and get your head round what's happened, instead of drowning yourself in drink.'

Fawles wasn't particularly used to being told how to behave, and attempted to snatch the tumbler from my hands.

As I tried to resist, the glass slipped from our fingers and shattered on the floor.

We stared at each other like a couple of idiots. We didn't look like a pair of dickheads or anything. Nope, not one bit . . .

Refusing to lose face, Fawles grabbed his bottle of whisky and took a swig straight from it.

He stepped forward to slide open the glazed door for Bronco, and took the opportunity to go out to the terrace and sit down in a wicker chair.

'But how could Mathilde Monney have got hold of them? There's just no way,' he wondered out loud.

His look of astonishment had given way to anxiety.

'Who's this woman you were writing to, Nathan?' I asked, joining him outside. 'Who's S.?'

'A woman I loved.'

'Yes, I guessed as much, but what happened to her?'

'She's dead.'

'Oh, I'm so sorry. Honestly.'

I sat down beside him in one of the armchairs.

'She was murdered in cold blood twenty years ago.'

'By whom?'

'A bastard of the worst possible kind.'

'Is that why you gave up writing?'

'Yes, as I began to explain to you this morning. I was in pieces. Broken by grief. I stopped because I'd lost all sense of clarity, all coherence in my thinking. And that's essential for being a writer.'

He gazed at the horizon, as though searching for answers. At night, when the surface of the water glittered below the full moon, the place was even more magical. You really had the feeling you were the only person on earth.

'It was a mistake to stop writing,' he continued, as if he'd just had a sudden revelation. 'Writing structures your life and your ideas, and it often ends up bringing order to the chaos of existence.'

A question had been nagging at me for a little while.

'Why have you never left this house?'

Fawles gave a deep sigh.

'I bought The Southern Cross for her, for this woman. She'd fallen in love with the island while falling in love with me. I guess staying here was like staying with her.'

I was dying to ask a thousand questions, but Fawles didn't give me the chance to ask them.

'I'll run you back in the car,' he said, leaping to his feet.

'There's no need, I've got my scooter. Go and rest instead.'

'OK, fine. Listen, Raphaël, you need to carry on digging into Mathilde Monney's motives. I can't explain why, but I have a hunch she's lying. There's something we're missing.'

He handed me his precious Bara No Niwa – which probably cost as much as my rent for a year – and I took a swig for the road, straight from the bottle like him.

'Why won't you tell me everything?'

'Because I still don't know the whole truth. And because ignorance is a kind of shield.'

'I can't believe you're saying that. Is ignorance really worth more than knowledge?'

'That's not what I said, and you know that very well. Trust me, I've been around: sometimes it's better not to know.'

9

THE DEATH OF OUR LOVED ONES

Thursday, 11 October 2018

1.

It was 6 a.m. It was still dark, but I pushed the shop door wide open to get some fresh air inside. Over by the desk, I inspected the bottom of the metal tin that normally contained ground coffee. It was empty. I should say that I'd already drunk around a dozen cups during a heavy night of research. Audibert's old printer was also just about to give up the ghost. I'd used the last ink cartridge we had in stock so I could keep a written record of my key findings, and then pinned all the documents and photos to the noticeboard.

I'd been surfing from site to site all night long, searching for information on the Verneuil murders. I'd raked through the online archives for the major newspapers, downloaded a few e-books and listened to extracts from several podcasts. It was easy to get bitten by the Verneuil bug. The story was both tragic and utterly compelling. To begin with, I'd thought I could come to a quick conclusion regarding the matter, but after an entire night immersed in the facts, I was still just as baffled. Several features made this incident rather disturbing. One of them being that they'd never tracked down the Verneuil family's killer, or killers. However, this affair wasn't some obscure, provincial cold case from the 1970s, but rather a full-blown mass murder which had unfolded in the very heart of Paris, at the turn of the twenty-first century. A massacre involving the family of a public figure, with the investigation being led by the elite of the French police. This was more of a Tarantino than a Claude Chabrol.

I'd done the maths: I was six when these events had taken place, so I had no memory of following the case on the news. But I was sure I'd vaguely heard mention of it afterwards, perhaps when I was a student or – more likely – watching *Bring in the Accused*, or listening to *The Crime Hour*.

Born in 1954 in Arcueil, Alexandre Verneuil had trained as a doctor, specialising in abdominal surgery. He'd started to become politically aware in senior school, in the wake of the civil unrest of May 1968, before forging links with the younger supporters of Michel Rocard and joining the Socialist Party. After completing his studies, he'd worked in two Paris hospitals, first at the Salpêtrière and then at the Cochin. His political commitment had subsequently morphed into a philanthropic one. His career path was similar to that of many other leading figures at the time who – finding themselves at the crossroads of civil society, humanitarian causes and politics – had steered their lives in a new direction. Working with Médecins du Monde and the

French Red Cross, Alexandre Verneuil was active in most theatres of war throughout the 1980s and 1990s, including Ethiopia, Afghanistan, Somalia, Rwanda and Bosnia. Following the Socialists' victory in the French parliamentary elections of 1997, he had been appointed as an advisor on health to the office of the secretary of state for international co-operation, but had only occupied the post for a few months, preferring instead to return to the field, and in particular to Kosovo. On returning to France at the end of 1999, he had become director of the School of Surgery for AP-HP, the trust in charge of university hospitals in Paris. Alongside his medical work, he had written several authoritative – and highly regarded – books on subjects including bioethics, the right of intervention and social exclusion. A respected name in humanitarian circles, Verneuil was also the darling of the media, who simply adored his fiery nature and his eloquence.

2.

The tragedy had played out during the evening of 11 June 2000, the day of the French football team's first match in the European Championships. That night, Verneuil and his wife Sofia – a dental surgeon whose practice on Rue Rocher was one of the most successful in Paris – were celebrating their son Théo's eleventh birthday. The family lived in a beautiful apartment in the 16th arrondissement, on Boulevard de Beauséjour, on the second floor of a 1930s building which offered superb views of the Eiffel Tower and the Jardin du Ranelagh. The photos of the kid I'd seen on the internet had unsettled me from the start, as he reminded me of myself at his age: a cheery face, a gap between his front teeth, a shock of blond hair and round, colourful glasses.

Eighteen years after it all happened, the precise sequence of events was still a matter of some debate. What did we know for certain? We knew that around a quarter past midnight, cops from the Anti-Crime Squad (the Paris night unit, BAC 75N), who'd been alerted by a neighbour from the adjoining block, had turned up at the Verneuils' home. The door to the apartment was open. Near the entrance, they'd had to step over the body of Alexandre Verneuil, lying on the floor, his face almost completely ripped off by a shot fired at point-blank range. His wife, Sofia, had been gunned down a little further away, in the kitchen doorway, killed by a bullet straight through the heart. As for young Théo, he'd been executed with a shot in his back and collapsed in the corridor. Pure, unmitigated horror.

What time had the carnage taken place? Probably around 11.45 p.m. At 11.30 p.m., Alexandre had called his father for a post-mortem on the football match (a 3–0 victory for the French team and the 'Zidane generation' against Denmark). He had hung up at 11.38 p.m. The neighbour had raised the alarm some twenty minutes later. By his own admission, he'd been slow to inform the police because, he thought, the festive atmosphere surrounding the match celebrations might have made him confuse gunfire with the sound of firecrackers.

The investigation had been no slipshod operation. Alexandre was the son of Patrice Verneuil, a former 'top cop' who had been co-director of the Paris Serious Crime Unit and who, at the time, was still a senior civil servant in the

Ministry of the Interior. The inquiries hadn't led to very much. They had revealed that a burglary had taken place that same night on the third – and uppermost – floor of the building, at the home of a retired couple who were in the south of France at the time. They had also noted the disappearance of Sofia Verneuil's jewellery and her husband's collection of watches (the doctor had been one of those champagne socialists, an unapologetic member of the 'Rolex left', and owned some priceless timepieces including a Paul Newman 'Panda' model valued at more than 500,000 francs).

The entrance to the building was fitted with a surveillance camera, but it hadn't been possible to use the footage. Its lens had shifted, so the device had ended up filming nothing but the wall in the hallway, and no one knew for certain if this was deliberate or accidental – nor whether this had happened just a few hours or several days earlier. Ballistics had identified the weapon used in the massacre: a pump-action shotgun with a rifled barrel which fired 12-bore cartridges (the most common), but which hadn't been recovered. Neither could analysis of the cartridge cases link them to any weapon already identified in connection with another incident. It was the same with the traces of DNA, which either belonged to the family or didn't match any of the profiles registered in various databases. And that was all. Or just about.

Trawling through these documents, it had dawned on me that I was among the first now able to revisit the affair in light of the possible role played by Apolline Chapuis and Karim Amrani. From that moment on, one particular scenario seemed more likely than most: the two criminals had started by burgling the unoccupied third-floor apartment belonging to the retired couple before coming down to break into the one below. Maybe they had thought the whole family would be away. But the Verneuils had surprised them. In a blind panic, Karim or Apolline had opened fire – one body, then two, then three – before making off with the watches, the jewellery and the camera.

This theory held water. All the articles I'd read about the 'Bonnie and Clyde of Stalingrad' suggested that Karim was violent. He hadn't hesitated to shoot at the owner of the bar-cum-betting shop, admittedly using only a shot pistol, but the poor guy had still lost an eye in the incident.

I stretched out in my seat and gave a yawn. I was going to take a shower, but I still had one podcast left to listen to: *Delicate Matters*, a programme broadcast on France Inter, had devoted one of its editions to the Verneuil case. I tried to launch the programme on my laptop, but the player simply kept on buffering and refused to load.

Shit, the internet's screwed up again . . .

This was an ongoing problem in the house. You frequently had to go upstairs to restart the router. The problem being that it had only just gone 6 a.m., and I didn't want to wake Audibert up. However, I decided to take the risk and tip-toed cautiously up the stairs. The bookseller was sleeping with his door ajar. I went into the living room, switched on the torch in my phone and crept as quietly as possible to the router sitting on top of the sideboard. I switched the device on and off, and then retreated hastily, trying not to make the wooden floor creak.

The hairs on my neck stood up. I had been here plenty of times before, but bizarrely, in the semi-darkness, I saw the room in a different light. I flashed my torch along the shelves of the bookcase. Sitting next to sumptuous Pléiade editions and books bound in artistic Bonet-Prassinos covers were several photos in wooden frames. Intuition? Instinct? Curiosity? I edged closer to take a good look at the family snaps. Firstly, pictures of Audibert and his wife Anita who, he'd told me during our first conversation, had died from cancer two years earlier. The two of them were captured at various stages of their lives. Their marriage in the mid-1960s, followed swiftly by a baby in their arms who turned into a sullen pre-teenage girl in another photo. In the early 1980s, the couple posed, all smiles, in front of the bonnet of a Citroën BX; then a trip to Greece ten years later, and another to New York before the fall of the Twin Towers. Those happy days, the ones you don't fully appreciate until they've gone. But it was the last two framed pictures that made my blood run cold. Two family photos in which I recognised other faces.

Faces that belonged to Alexandre, Sofia and Théo Verneuil.

And Mathilde Monney.

3.

The ringing of the phone wrenched Fawles out of a fitful, tormented sleep. He had dozed off in his armchair with Bronco at his feet. The writer yawned, stood up with some difficulty and dragged himself to the receiver.

'Hello?'

His voice sounded lifeless, as if his vocal cords had rusted during the night. His neck was stiff and numb, and he felt as though the slightest movement would make his body creak.

It was Sabina Benoit, the former manager of the library at the Youth Care Centre.

'Nathan, I know it's very early, but since you asked me to call you as soon as I had any news—'

'You did the right thing,' replied Fawles.

'I've managed to get the list of patients who were at your talk. In fact, you came to speak twice, once on 20 March 1998, and then again on 24 June the same year.'

'And?'

'There was no Mathilde Monney among the girls who attended.'

Fawles sighed and rubbed his eyes. Why would the journalist have lied to him on this point?

'The only Mathilde who was there was called Mathilde Verneuil.'

Fawles felt a chill run down his spine.

'She was the daughter of that poor Dr Verneuil,' continued the librarian. 'I can still picture her now: pretty, reserved, sensitive, intelligent . . . Who could have known, back then, that something so dreadful would happen to her?'

4.

Mathilde was Alexandre Verneuil's daughter and the grand-daughter of Grégoire Audibert! Stunned by this revelation, I stood there for a good minute, stock-still in the dark. Dumb-founded. Blown to shreds. Goosebumps all over, frozen to the spot.

I couldn't leave it there. On the top shelves of the book-case I found some photo albums. Four thick volumes bound in cloth covers, organised by decade. I sat cross-legged on the floor and, by the light of my torch, began to flick through them, looking at the pictures, skimming over the notes and captions. I gleaned a few key facts, which could be summed up in a handful of dates. Grégoire and Anita Audibert had had only one child – a daughter, Sofia, born in 1962, who had married Alexandre Verneuil in 1982. Their marriage had produced Mathilde and Théo who, during their childhood, had frequently visited the Isle of Beaumont on holiday.

How could Fawles and I possibly have missed that? It seemed to me that none of the articles I'd read had ever mentioned Mathilde. As I had my phone in my hand, I did a quick check by typing some keywords into Google. An open-access article from *L'Express* dating back to July 2000 said that 'the family's eldest child, a girl aged sixteen, wasn't in Paris on the night of the tragedy, as she was revising for her French baccalaureate at a friend's house in Normandy.'

A host of theories were swimming around in my brain. I felt I had just taken a critical step forward in the investigation, but the full implications of what I'd discovered still eluded me. I wasn't sure if I should leave. From where I was, I could hear Audibert, who was sleeping in the room next door, and his even, regular snoring. Perhaps I'd already pushed my luck as far as it would go. But equally, perhaps there were still secrets left for me to unearth. I risked a quick peek in his room. It was an ascetic, practically monastic interior. Near the bed, on a little desk pushed right up against the wall, a laptop was the sole concession to modernity. In my excitement I threw caution to the wind. It was tempting fate, but I just *had* to find out more. I went up to the desk and, almost despite myself, felt my fingers closing around the computer.

5.

Once back on the ground floor, I worked as fast as I could to access the content on his device. Audibert certainly wasn't familiar with the latest technology, but he wasn't as much of a Luddite as he liked to make out. His laptop was a good old VAIO notebook from the end of the 2000s. I was pretty sure of one thing: the password for unlocking it had to be same as the one for the PC in the shop. I gave it a shot, only to discover that . . . yes, this was indeed the case.

The hard disk was virtually empty. I had no idea what I was looking for, but I was now completely convinced that there was more information waiting to be found. There were just a few office folders, containing items no one had looked at for ages: an out-of-date version of the shop accounts, the odd invoice or two, a topographical map of Beaumont and some PDFs of press articles concerning the criminal past of Apolline Chapuis and Karim Amrani. Nothing new, I'd read them all before. They merely showed that Audibert had carried out the same research as I had. I hesitated about digging around in his emails or messages. Audibert didn't have a personal Facebook page, but he had set up one for the shop which hadn't been updated for more than a year. As for the laptop's photo library, it didn't hold a great deal – but it did have three photo albums. Their contents would prove to be explosive.

Firstly, there were numerous screenshots from Apolline Chapuis's website, and then, in another folder, the pictures of Karim Amrani strolling around Évry taken with a telephoto lens. The same ones I'd found in Mathilde's room. But that wasn't the end of my surprises, as the last folder contained yet more snaps. Initially, I thought they were the ones Mathilde had shown Fawles: the two petty criminals on their trip to Hawaii and Théo Verneuil's birthday celebrations. However, it was clear that Mathilde had only shown the writer a selection of photos from that evening. Other images proved, in fact, that the young girl really had been there for her brother's birthday, on that fateful night when her family had been killed.

My eyes were stinging, my head was buzzing and I could feel the blood thumping in my temples. How could this fact have escaped the attention of the investigators? I was gripped by a strange sense of fear, unable to look away from the screen which was burning the back of my eyes. At sixteen, Mathilde appeared in the photos as a slightly fragile, pretty girl, with her mind elsewhere, a forced smile and a fleeting look of sadness on her face.

All manner of hypotheses, horribly warped and twisted ones, ran through my mind. The most soul-destroying of these being that Mathilde might have murdered her family. The final photo in the digital album held yet another surprise. It was dated 3 May 2000 – undoubtedly taken during the May Day long weekend. There were Mathilde and Théo, posing with their grandparents in front of The Scarlet Rose.

I was about to close the laptop when, just to make certain, I took a quick look in the recycle bin. It contained two video

159

files, which I first dragged back onto the desktop and then onto my USB stick. I plugged in my headphones before playing the recordings.

And what I saw chilled me to the bone.

6.

Sitting in his kitchen, elbows on the table and head in his hands, Fawles was reflecting on the consequences of what Sabina Benoit had told him. Monney had to be a false name. Mathilde Monney wasn't Swiss and her name was in fact Mathilde Verneuil. And if this young girl really was Alexandre Verneuil's daughter, everything that had happened on the island in recent days took on a new meaning.

Because of his loathing for the media, Fawles hadn't seen any of this coming. The fact that Mathilde was a journalist had thrown him, and led him astray right from the beginning. In truth, Mathilde was only on the island for one simple reason: to avenge the massacre of her family. The theory that she was the one who'd killed Karim and Apolline – whom she'd identified as her parents' murderers – was now highly credible.

A flood of images, and memories, and faint, crackling sounds surged through Fawles's brain. From the depths of this jumbled, seething mass, a single picture came into focus. One of the photos from the birthday evening which Mathilde had shown him on the boat: Verneuil, his wife and little Théo posing on their terrace, with the Eiffel Tower behind them. He was struck by the blindingly obvious: the fact that this three-quarter shot existed meant someone must have taken it. And there was every chance that person was Mathilde. The girl who, on the night of the massacre, was most probably in the family apartment too.

Suddenly, a pall of darkness descended on Fawles, as black as the polar night. Now he knew everything – and he could sense he was in great danger.

He quickly got up to return to the living room. At the back of the room, beside the metal racks that served as log holders, was the cabinet carved from olive wood where he kept his shotgun. He opened the door. Only to find the weapon was no longer where it should have been. Someone had made off with the gun engraved with the kulshedra. That damned gun. The one behind all those atrocities. The one that lay at the root of all his misery. Then he remembered the old rule of storytelling: if a novelist refers to the existence of a weapon at the start of their narrative, then it's a given that a shot will be fired and one of the protagonists is sure to die at the end of the book.

As he believed in the laws of fiction, Fawles was convinced he was going to die.

That very day.

7.

I played the first video. It was five minutes long, and must have been filmed with a mobile phone, in a place that appeared to be someone's house.

'For God's sake! I don't know anything . . . I've already told you everything, I don't know any more!'

With his hands bound in handcuffs, and his arms pinned down above his head, Karim was lying on a sort of low table that sloped towards the floor.

From his swollen face and bloody mouth, you could tell he'd just been subjected to an absolute hammering. The man conducting the interrogation was a tall guy I'd never seen in my life. Grey-haired and with an impressive physique, he was wearing a checked shirt, a Barbour jacket and a tartan cap.

I moved closer to the screen to take a better look at him. How old was he? At least seventy-five, going by the wrinkles on his face and his general appearance. He was finding it rather awkward to move around, because of his massive paunch, but he was built like a bulldozer, sweeping aside everything in his path.

'I don't know any more!' yelled Karim.

The old guy didn't seem to be listening to him. He vanished from the screen for a few seconds before reappearing with a towel which he spread over the ex-dealer's face. Then, with all the diligence of an expert torturer, he began pouring water onto the cloth.

That despicable form of torture known as waterboarding.

Watching the film was unbearable. The old guy carried on to the point where Karim was suffocating. His body stiffened, then contorted, writhing and convulsing. When he removed the towel at last, I thought Karim wouldn't come round again. A mixture of bubbles, foam and bile spewed from his mouth, like a geyser. He remained lifeless for a moment, and finally vomited before mumbling:

'I . . . I've fucking told you everything . . .'

The old guy tilted the table and whispered in Karim's ear:

'Well then, you'll just have to start over, from the beginning!'

The man was gasping for air. The terror was plain to see on his face.

'I don't know any more.'

'Fine, so if you won't, I'll start instead, shall I?'

And the old guy grabbed hold of the towel again.

'No!' screamed Karim.

He somehow managed to catch his breath and tried to gather his thoughts.

'That night, 11 June 2000, Apolline and me, we went to the 16th arrondissement. Number 39 Boulevard de Beauséjour. We went to break into the old toffs' place on the third floor. We'd had a solid tip-off that they wouldn't be in the apartment.'

'Who gave you the tip-off?'

'Dunno. Must've been my gang at the time. The old couple were meant to be loaded, but most of the cash and the jewellery turned out to be in a built-in safe, set in concrete. No way we could nick it.'

He was speaking rapidly, monotonously, as if he'd already told this story countless times. His voice was distorted by his broken nose, and blood was dripping down his eyelids which were so badly bruised he couldn't open them.

'We pinched a few trinkets – you know, stuff that's easy to flog. Then, when we were just about to get the hell out, we heard shots, coming from below.'

'How many?'

'Three. We were scared stiff, so we hid in one of the

163

bedrooms. We waited for quite a bit – we were terrified of the cops, we knew they'd turn up any minute, but at the same time we were freaking out cos some guy was blowing folk to bits on the second floor.'

'You didn't see who it was?'

'No! We were shitting ourselves, I keep telling you. We let several minutes go by, cos we didn't dare go down. We tried our best to get out through the roof, but the hatch was locked. So there was nothing for it – we had to take the stairs.'

'And then?'

'When we got to the second floor, Apolline was still scared to death. I was feeling a lot better. I'd sniffed a line of coke in the old folk's bedroom. I was completely stoned – practically euphoric. We got to the door and I poked my head through the opening. It was carnage, total carnage. There was blood all over the place and three bodies slumped on the floor. Apolline screamed and ran off, she said she'd wait for me in the car park, under the building.'

'Don't worry, we'll grill your little girlfriend too.'

'She's not my girlfriend. We've not spoken for eighteen years.'

'So what did you do in the Verneuils' apartment?'

'They were all dead, I told you. I went into the living room and then the bedrooms. And I nabbed anything I could – some posh watches, loads of cash, jewellery, a camera . . . Then I left to catch up with Apolline. We buggered off to Hawaii a few weeks later, and that's where we lost that fucking camera.'

'Yep, that was bloody stupid,' said the old guy, seeming to agree.

He gave a long sigh – and suddenly jabbed his elbow violently into Karim's ribs.

'The worst part is, it wasn't just the camera you lost that day. It was your life too.'

And he hurled himself at him, mad with rage, his enormous fists pounding away with the most incredible force you could imagine.

I was horrified. It felt as though the blood were about to spatter onto my face. I looked away from the screen. I was quaking, as if I had a fever. I was trembling all over. Who was this man, capable of killing with his bare hands? What lay behind the insanity that had taken hold of him?

The place was freezing. I got up to close the bookshop door. For the first time ever, I physically felt my life was in danger. I agonised for a split second about making a run for it, taking the laptop with me, but curiosity drove me back behind the desk to play the second video.

I hoped it would be less gruesome, but that wasn't the case. It featured an identical scene of extreme torture, ending in death. This time, it was Apolline playing the part of the victim along with, in the role of the torturer, a man seen only from behind. He was wearing a tight-fitting dark raincoat, and looked younger and less heavily built than Karim's murderer. The film was of a much lower quality, most probably due to the enclosed space which was poorly lit. A poky little room, all filthy and shabby, where you could just make out grey walls of exposed stone.

Apolline was tied to a chair. Her face was covered in blood, some of her teeth were broken and one eye was severely bashed up. Her abuser, armed with a poker, had probably been torturing her for quite some time. The film was short, and her story appeared to tally with Karim's.

'I was scared shitless, believe me! I never went into the Verneuils' apartment. I got the hell out – I went straight down to the car park, to wait for Karim.'

She sniffed and shook her head to dislodge a lock of hair, stuck together with blood, that kept falling onto her eyes.

'I was convinced the cops were going to show up. To be honest, I was surprised they weren't there already. It was pitch black down there. I was huddled up between a concrete post and a van. But all of a sudden the lights went on, and a car came up from the lower level.'

Apolline's voice was quavering, choked with terror and pain, but the man with the poker forced her to keep going.

'It was a grey Porsche, with red and blue stripes. It stopped in front of me for a good thirty seconds, because the shutter wasn't working. It got stuck, halfway up.'

'Who was inside the Porsche?'

'Two men.'

'Two? Are you sure?'

'Positive. I didn't see the passenger's face, but the man who was driving got out. He went to fix the shutter.'

'Did you know him?'

'Not personally, but I'd seen him before, doing an interview on TV. And I'd read one of his books too.'

'One of his books?'

'Yes, it was that author. Nathan Fawles.'

THE UNSPEAKABLE TRUTH

10

WRITERS AGAINST THE REST OF THE WORLD

1.

It was that author. Nathan Fawles.

Those had been Apolline's last words before she died. The video rolled on for a few more seconds, showing her slipping into a coma, and then succumbing to a final blow from the poker.

Beyond the revelation itself – which had thrown me into a terrible state of confusion – I was preoccupied by a far more pressing question: what the fuck were these films doing on Audibert's laptop?

I could sense my excitement building, despite the horrific nature of the scene, and in a feverish haze I sat through the video of Apolline's execution a second time. This time I took off my headphones to focus on the setting. *Those rubble-stone walls* . . . I had seen walls just like them, when taking boxes of books down to the cellar of The Scarlet Rose in the goods lift. Or maybe I'd been imagining things . . .

The bunch of keys for the shop included those for the basement. I'd been down there two or three times, but never noticed anything particularly suspicious.

I decided to have another look around, even though my heart was pounding. There was no question, however, of using the lift which made one hell of a racket. I went out into the little internal courtyard, where there was a trapdoor giving access to the cellar. It opened onto a wooden staircase as steep as a ladder. As soon as I stepped onto it, I was struck by the unpleasant smell of damp.

When I reached the bottom I switched on the fluorescent tube which produced a flickering glow, revealing nothing but shelves thick with cobwebs and boxes packed with books on the verge of going mouldy. The neon light fizzled and crackled for a few seconds, before it suddenly went out with a crisp snap.

Shit . . .

I took out my phone to use as a torch, but tripped over a rusty old air conditioner lying on the floor. I tumbled onto the concrete and found myself rolling around in the dust.

Nice one, Rafa . . .

I rescued my phone and got back on my feet before plunging into the shadows. The space was long and narrow, and much bigger than I'd imagined. At the back of the basement, I could make out the sound of a fan, similar to a heating unit or an exhaust vent. The humming came from a tangle of pipes which disappeared behind three wooden decking panels stacked vertically against the wall, one in front of the other.

I wondered where these pipes went. After struggling away at the panels for a good minute or so, I managed to shift them and discovered another entrance. A kind of sliding metal door, like something you'd find on the side of an industrial oven. It was secured with a lock, but I had the key for this too, on the same impressive bunch that belonged to Audibert.

Feeling sick with fear, I rushed through the opening, and emerged in a curious little room which contained a DIY workbench and a chest freezer. I spotted the poker I'd seen in the video lying on the bench, along with a rusty hammer with sharp corners, a dark wooden mallet and stonemason's chisels . . .

A noose tightened around my chest. I was shaking all over. When I opened the freezer, I couldn't hold back a scream. The inside had been repainted. With blood.

I'm living with a fucking nutter.

I turned round and fled, shooting back up to the courtyard like a rocket.

It was Audibert who had tortured Apolline Chapuis to death, and there was no doubt he'd kill me too if I didn't get out pretty damn quick. Back inside the shop, I could hear the wooden floor squeaking upstairs. He had just got up. First the sound of footsteps, then boards creaking on the staircase. *Fuck* . . . In a flash, I stuffed Audibert's laptop into my backpack before slamming the door and jumping on my scooter.

2.

The sky was streaked with long bands of cloud, pierced by the dawn light. The road that ran along the shore was deserted. The smell of iodine floated up from the sea and

171

mingled with the scent of eucalyptus. I put my foot down – which simply meant that, even with the wind sweeping me along, I was still struggling to do forty-five kilometres an hour. Hardly Formula One. Every couple of minutes, I would steal a worried glance over my shoulder. I'd never feared so much for my life. It felt as though Audibert might appear at any moment – as if he were about to burst onto the Strada Principale, brandishing his poker and looking to get even with me.

What should I do? My instinctive reaction had been to seek refuge at Nathan's. But I couldn't pretend I was unaware of what I'd seen on the video, and the accusations levelled at him by Apolline Chapuis.

I was an easy target to manipulate. I'd always known Fawles wasn't telling me everything he knew about this business – and he himself had never tried to convince me otherwise. In rushing off to see him, I was potentially walking straight into the lion's den. I thought again about the pump-action shotgun with the rifled barrel which he kept close to hand. It was very likely this was the weapon used to massacre the Verneuils. For a good five minutes, it felt as though I were losing my bearings and then I pulled myself together again.

Although my mother had drummed into me that I mustn't trust a soul, I'd always ignored her orders and done precisely the opposite. My naivety had played tricks on me through-out my life, and I would always end up kicking myself afterwards, but I firmly believed that losing this sense of innocence would amount to losing my sense of who I was. So I decided to stick with my gut instinct: the man who had written *Loreleï Strange* and *Les Foudroyés* couldn't possibly be such a bastard.

When I turned up at The Southern Cross, Fawles looked as if he'd been awake for a long time. He was wearing a dark roll-neck jumper and a tan-coloured suede jacket. He seemed very relaxed, and twigged immediately that something serious had happened.

'You need to see this!' I blurted out, without even giving him time to calm me down.

I removed Audibert's laptop from my bag and played the two videos. Fawles watched them without showing the slightest hint of emotion, even when Apolline came out with his name.

'Do you know these two men, the ones torturing Amrani and Chapuis?'

'The first guy, I've no idea. The second, that's Grégoire Audibert. I found the freezer where he stashed Apolline's body in his cellar.'

Fawles remained stony-faced, but I could tell he was rattled.

'Did you know Mathilde was Audibert's granddaughter and Alexandre Verneuil's daughter?'

'I found out an hour ago.'

'Nathan, why would Apolline accuse you?'

'She's not accusing me. She's simply saying she saw me in a car along with another man.'

'Who was it? Just tell me you're innocent and I'll believe you.'

'It wasn't me who killed the Verneuils, I swear.'

'But you were in their apartment that awful night?'

'Yes, I was there, but I didn't kill them.'

'I don't get it!'

'One day, I'll tell you everything in detail, but not now.'

Fawles suddenly looked nervous. He was fiddling with a little remote – the size of a zapper for the garage – which he'd just taken from his pocket.

'Why not now?'

'Because you're in grave danger, Raphaël! We're not in a novel here, pal. These aren't empty words. Apolline and Karim are both dead, and their murderers are still on the loose. For some reason or other, which I still don't really get, the Verneuil affair's back in the spotlight. And no good can ever come of a tragedy like this.'

'What do you want me to do?'

'You're getting off the island. Right now!' he said crisply, looking at his watch. 'The ferry starts running again at 8 a.m. I'll give you a lift.'

'Seriously?'

Fawles pointed at the laptop.

'You've seen the videos. We both have. Those people are capable of anything.'

'But—'

'Quick, let's go!' he said, grabbing me by the arm.

With Bronco at my side, I followed the writer to his car. The Mini Moke – which must have been standing idle for several weeks – initially refused to start. Just when I thought Fawles had flooded the engine, he gave it one last try and, miraculously, it sprang into life. The dog leapt in the back and the doorless convertible – a horrendously uncomfortable thing, I soon discovered – juddered along through the trees, following the dirt road before it eventually joined the main one.

The journey to the ferry was hard going. The feeble dawn light had surrendered to an onslaught of grey. Now the sky was cluttered with dark, sooty clouds, as if someone had rubbed over it with a blunt piece of charcoal. The wind too had picked up, whipping against our poor little windscreen. This was not the east wind, gentle and moist, nor the familiar mistral which swept away the clouds to leave fresh blue skies. This was icy and bitter, a polar wind, laden with its quota of thunder and lightning: the black mistral.

When we arrived at the harbour, it felt as though I'd landed in a ghost town. Thick blankets of mist floated over the cobbles. Ribbons of pearly-white haze swirled around the street signs and lampposts, and obscured the boats moored by the quayside. A real pea-souper. Fawles parked in front of the harbour master's cabin and went to buy my ticket himself. Then he walked me up to the ferry.

'Why don't you come with me, Nathan?' I asked, stepping onto the gangplank of the boat. 'You're in danger too, aren't you?'

He remained on the quay with his dog, and declined my offer with a shake of his head.

'Take care of yourself, Raphaël.'

'Come with me!' I begged.

'I can't. If you start a fire you have to put it out too. I need to put an end to something.'

'What?'

'The devastation caused by a hideous machine. A machine I set in motion twenty years ago.'

He waved at me and I knew I wouldn't learn any more. As I gazed at him walking away with his dog, I suddenly had goosebumps all over and was overcome by a deep sense of sadness, because something told me this was the last time

I would ever see Nathan Fawles. But then, abruptly, he doubled back. He looked benevolently into my eyes and, to my astonishment, handed me the corrected manuscript of my novel which he'd rolled up to make it fit in the pocket of his sailing jacket.

'You know, *Crown Shyness* is a good novel, Raphaël. It deserves to be published, even without my corrections.'

'That's not what publishers who've read it think.'

He shook his head and heaved a sigh filled with contempt:

'Publishers . . . Publishers are people who'd like you to be grateful to them for telling you what they think of your book in a couple of sentences, while you've been slaving away for two years to make it hang together. People who sit around having lunch until three in restaurants in Midtown or Saint-Germain-des-Prés, while you're burning your eyes out in front of your screen, but who'll call you every day if you're late signing their contract. People who'd like to be Max Perkins or Gordon Lish, but who'll never be anything but themselves: admin folk who merely handle literature, reading your manuscripts through the lens of an Excel spreadsheet. People for whom you can never work fast enough, who treat you like a kid, who always know better than you what people want to read, or what makes a good title or a good cover. People who, once you've become successful, often *despite* them, will tell everyone they "made" you. The same people who told Simenon that Maigret was "sickeningly banal", who turned down *Carrie*, *Harry Potter* and *Loreleï Strange*—'

I cut Fawles short in the middle of his rant.

'*Loreleï Strange* was rejected?'

'I've not gone bragging about it, but yes. *Loreleï* was turned down by fourteen agents and publishers. Including the one who ended up publishing it later, thanks to the efforts of Jasper Van Wyck. That's why you mustn't give too much importance to those guys.'

'Nathan, once this business is all over, will you help me get *Crown Shyness* published? Will you help me become a writer?'

For the first time – and the last – I saw Fawles break into a broad smile, and what he said confirmed my first impression of him. The one I'd always had.

'You don't need my help, Raphaël. You're *already* a writer.'

He gave me a friendly thumbs up before turning around and heading back to his car.

3.

The fog was getting thicker and thicker. The *Audacious* was three-quarters full, but I'd managed to find a seat inside. Through the window of the ferry I could make out the last few passengers emerging from the mist, scurrying to get on board.

I was still in shock from what Fawles had said to me, but I also had a bad taste in my mouth. The taste of defeat. The sense of deserting the battlefield in the heat of combat. I had arrived on Beaumont brimming with fire and passion, under the triumphant rays of the sun, and I was leaving the island in the rain, sheepish and fearful, in the face of impending danger, just as the final act was about to be written.

I thought about my second novel, already well under

way. *The Secret Life of Writers.* I was a living, breathing person in this tale. I was one of the characters on the page. The narrator of my story couldn't simply run away from a war zone like a coward just when things were getting serious. An opportunity like this would never arise again. But then I remembered the warning Fawles had given me. 'You're in grave danger, Raphaël! We're not in a novel here, pal.' Except that Fawles probably didn't believe those words himself. And wasn't that precisely what he'd advised me to do anyway, to add a dash of the novel to my life – and a dash of life to my writing? I was hooked on this kind of thing – those moments when fiction and reality start bleeding into each other. That was part of the reason I loved reading so much. It wasn't about escape – forsaking real life in favour of imaginary worlds – but rather returning to my own world transformed by my reading. I would emerge all the richer for my travels and encounters in fiction, and eager to plough those riches back into real life.

And then there was Nathan Fawles. My hero, my mentor. The man who, five minutes before, had dubbed me one of his own. I couldn't possibly leave him to face mortal danger all by himself. Fuck it, I was made of stronger stuff! I wasn't a kid. I was a writer who was about to help another one.

Two writers against the whole world . . .

As I was getting up from my seat to return to the deck, I spotted Audibert's mini-van pulling up in front of the town hall. An old Renault 4, repainted in duck green, which he'd told me he'd bought from a florist a few years earlier.

The bookseller double-parked in front of the post office

and got out to drop an envelope into the letterbox. He then walked briskly back to his vehicle, but before getting behind the wheel, he paused and took a long look at the ferry. I hid behind a metal pole, hoping he hadn't seen me. By the time I stepped out again, the van had already turned the corner. However, I thought I could still make out its lights flashing through the mist, as though it had come to a halt.

What should I do? I was torn between fear and the desire to get to the heart of this. I was also worried about Nathan. Now that I knew what Audibert was capable of, did I have the right to abandon Fawles? A blast on the ferry's foghorn signalled we were about to leave. *Make up your mind!* Just as the boat was casting off, I jumped back onto the wooden walkway. I couldn't run away. Leaving would be like demeaning myself, and giving up all I believed in.

I walked along the quay past the harbour master's office, and then crossed the road towards the post office. The mist was everywhere. I followed the pavement to Rue Mortevielle where Audibert's van had turned.

The street was deserted, submerged in a damp, foggy syrup. The closer I came to the vehicle, with its blinkers piercing through the haze, the more it felt as if some unseen beast were circling around me, poised to swallow me up. When I got to the window, I found there was no one at the wheel.

'Looking for me, Fakespeare?'

I whirled around to discover a figure wrapped in a black raincoat. It was Audibert. I opened my mouth to yell, but before I could make any sound at all, he slammed his poker down on me with all the force he could muster. A scream of sheer terror remained stuck in my throat.

And everything around me went black.

4.

The rain was pelting down.

Nathan Fawles had left in such a rush that the house had been left open to the elements. When he returned to The Southern Cross, he didn't bother closing the gate behind him. The enemy he had to confront wasn't the kind you could fend off by erecting barriers or locking yourself away.

He went out onto the terrace to secure one of the shutters which was banging against the wall. Battered by the wind and rain, Beaumont now looked completely different. You were no longer in the Mediterranean, but on a Scottish island being pounded by a storm.

Fawles stood completely still for several minutes, letting the warm raindrops hammer against his body. He was bombarded by an endless succession of harrowing images. The massacre of the Verneuil family. Karim being tortured. Apolline's execution. His head was also throbbing with words from the letters he'd reread the day before. Letters written twenty years earlier to the woman he had loved so much. His world had been torn apart, and tears streamed down his cheeks as everything surged back to the surface. The fury of having missed out on love. The life he had given up. That crimson line, traced out in the blood of so many corpses – collateral victims in a story where they were merely shadowy extras.

He went back inside to change. As he was putting on dry clothes, he suddenly felt incredibly weary, as if all the sap that once raced through his veins had drained away. He was desperate for all this to be over. He had lived these last twenty years like a samurai. He had tried to face up to life with courage and honour. To embrace self-discipline and follow a solitary path, which meant he was mentally prepared to meet his end and wouldn't be afraid when Death finally showed up.

He was ready. He would have preferred this final chapter not to be written amid the sound and the fury, but that would be hoping in vain. He was fighting on the front line, in a battle where there would never be any victors. Only the dead.

For twenty years he had known things would end badly. That, sooner or later, he would be forced to kill or be killed, because that was in the very nature of the horrifying secret he had guarded for so long.

But, even in his darkest nightmares, Fawles had never imagined that when Death came to carry him off, it would possess the green eyes, the golden locks and the exquisite face of Mathilde Monney.

11

THE DARK NIGHT
OF THE SOUL

1.

When I regained consciousness, I was tied up in the back of
Audibert's Renault 4 and an invisible demon was scraping
the inside of my skull with a sharp object. I was in agony. I
had a broken nose, I couldn't open my left eye and blood was
gushing from my eyebrow. I panicked, and tried to wrig-
gle free, but the bookseller had bound my wrists and ankles
tightly with bungee cords.

'Let me go, Audibert!'

'Shut the fuck up, you little prick!'

The van's wipers were struggling to clear away the tor-
rents of water lashing against the windscreen. I couldn't see
very much, but I could tell we were driving eastwards, heading for Le Safranier Point.

'Why are you doing this?'

'Shut up, I said!'

I was drenched in a mixture of rain and sweat. My knees

were shaking and my heart was racing. I was scared to death
– but despite everything, I was desperate to know what had
happened.

'So *you* were the first to get those pictures from the old
camera, weren't you? It wasn't Mathilde!'

Audibert sniggered:

'They were sent to me via the shop's Facebook account,
can you believe it? That Yank from Alabama tracked me
down, thanks to the very first photo: Mathilde and me outside the bookshop, the day I gave her the camera for her
sixteenth birthday!'

I closed my eyes briefly to try to visualise the sequence of
events. So Audibert, then, had been the mastermind behind
a belated act of revenge, designed to make those who'd murdered his daughter, son-in-law and grandson pay for their
crimes. But I didn't get why he had dragged his granddaughter into his vendetta. When I said this, he turned his head
towards me and, spit drooling from his lips, showered me
with abuse:

'Do you really think I didn't try and protect her, you little
turd! I never showed her the photos. I only sent them to
Patrice Verneuil, her paternal grandfather.'

It was hard to think clearly, but I did recall coming across
Alexandre's father in my research during the night. Patrice
Verneuil, the former 'top cop' and co-director of the Serious
Crime Unit who, at the time of the affair, had been an advi-
sor in the Ministry of the Interior. Although sidelined under
Prime Minister Lionel Jospin, he had ended his career in a
blaze of glory when Nicolas Sarkozy became interior minis-
ter and consequently head of the French police.

'Patrice and I, we shared the same pain,' he carried on,

calming down a little. 'When Alexandre, Sofia and Théo were murdered, our lives came to a standstill. Or rather, our lives continued without us. Patrice's wife was heartbroken and committed suicide in 2002. My wife, Anita, kept up a brave face to the very end. But in hospital, just as she was dying, she kept on telling me, like a mantra, how much it pained her that those who'd murdered our children were still alive.'

His hands were clenched tightly around the steering wheel. He sounded as though he were talking to himself, and you could sense a controlled anger in his voice, primed and ready to explode.

'When I received those photos and showed them to Patrice, we immediately thought it was a gift from God, or the Devil, to allow us to satisfy our thirst for revenge. Patrice circulated pictures of the two little thugs among a few old-timers from Serious Crime, and they didn't take long to identify them.'

I tried again to set my hands free, but the bungee cords were cutting into my wrists.

'Of course, we decided to leave Mathilde out of our plans,' he went on. 'And we split the work between us. Patrice took care of Amrani, and my job was to lure Chapuis to the island by posing as the manager of the Gallinari wine estate.'

Carried away by his narrative, Audibert almost seemed to relish giving me details of his crime:

'I went to meet the little tart at the ferry exit. It was pouring down, like today. I gave her a good old zap with a taser in the van, and then I lugged her down to the cellar.'

2.

Now I was able to gauge just how much I had underestimated Audibert. He might look like an old provincial schoolteacher, but behind the mask lurked a cold-blooded killer. He and Patrice Verneuil had planned to film the interrogations so they could exchange them with each other.

'Once we'd got down to the basement,' he continued, 'I drained all the blood from her body. Every last drop. And I savoured every minute. But even that was too soft a punishment, given the hell she'd put us through.'

Why had I turned up in that alley feeling so naively optimistic? Fuck it, why hadn't I listened to Nathan?

'It was while she was being tortured that she finally came out with Fawles's name.'

'So, do you think Fawles killed the Verneuils?' I asked.

'Not in the least. I think that cunt Chapuis spat his name out at random, just because she was on Beaumont and the island's connected to the writer. I'm convinced they're guilty, the filthy vermin. Should've rotted away in prison, the bloody pair of them. In the end, they only got what they deserved. And if I could kill them again a second time, I'd do it with pleasure.'

'But then the matter's closed, because Apolline and Karim are dead.'

'For me it was, but that's not what that pig-headed Patrice thought. He was hell-bent on interrogating Fawles himself, but he died before he could do it.'

'Patrice Verneuil's dead?'

Audibert cackled like a lunatic.

'A fortnight ago. Eaten away by stomach cancer! And before breathing his last, that idiot couldn't find anything better to do than send Mathilde a USB stick containing the photos from the old camera, the videos and the results of our investigation!'

The pieces of the puzzle were falling into place, revealing a mind-blowing scenario.

'When she saw the photos of that evening, and the birthday celebration, Mathilde was devastated. For eighteen years, she'd suppressed the memory of being there, in the apartment, when her parents and brother were killed. She'd forgotten everything.'

'I find that hard to believe.'

'I don't give a shit what you believe! It's the truth. When she turned up at my place, ten days ago, Mathilde was beside herself, like a woman possessed, determined to avenge her family. Patrice had told her that Apolline's corpse was stashed away in my freezer.'

'She's the one who crucified the body, then? On the oldest eucalyptus on Beaumont?'

I saw Audibert nodding in the rear-view mirror.

'What for?'

'To trigger the blockade around the island, of course! To stop Nathan Fawles running away and force him to take responsibility for his actions.'

'But you just said you don't think Fawles is guilty!'

'No, but *she* thinks he is. And I want to protect my granddaughter.'

'Protect her how?'

He said nothing. Through the window, I saw we had just driven past Silver Cove Beach. I could feel my heart pounding frantically in my chest. Where was he taking me?

'Audibert, I saw you posting a letter a little while ago. What was that?'

'Ha! Been spying on me, nancy boy? It was a full confession, sent to the police station in Toulon. A letter in which I admit to murdering Apolline and Fawles.'

That's why we were driving towards The Southern Cross! Le Safranier Point was now less than a kilometre away. Audibert had decided Fawles had to be eliminated.

'You see, I have to kill him before Mathilde does.'

'And me?'

'You happened to be in the wrong place at the wrong time. They call that collateral damage. Bloody shame, isn't it?'

I had to try to stop this madman in his tracks. Despite my feet being trussed together, I gave the back of the driver's seat one hell of a kick. Audibert wasn't expecting me to lash out. He yelled and turned round to face me, just as a second kick landed squarely on his head.

'Fucking little fairy, I'll give you . . .'

The van swerved. Its metal roof echoed to the hammering of the rain and, as the water gushed overhead, I felt as though I were on a boat being swept away by the current.

'You're fucking dead, you little shit!' screamed Audibert, grabbing the poker lying on the passenger seat.

I thought he'd regained control of the vehicle, but a moment later the Renault 4 crashed through the safety barrier and tumbled into the void.

3.

I never thought I was really going to die. For the few seconds the van was falling through the air, I kept on hoping – right to the end – that something would happen to avoid a tragedy. Because life is a novel. And no author is going to kill off their narrator when there's seventy pages to go before the end of the story.

This moment doesn't taste of death, or fear. I don't see my life flashing before my eyes, like a film on fast-forward, nor does the scene unfold in slow motion, like Michel Piccoli's car accident in *The Things of Life*.

Nevertheless, something rather odd does pop into my head. A memory, or rather a secret my father shared with me a short time ago. An outpouring, as sudden as it was surprising. He told me how 'luminous' – that was his own word for it – his life had been when I was a child. *When you were little, we did loads of things together,* he reminded me. And that's true. I remember walks in the forest, visits to museums, going to the theatre, making models, DIY projects at home. But there was more. He was the one who took me to school every morning and, on the way, he'd always teach me a thing or two. It might be some historical event, a story related to art or artists, a grammatical rule, a little lesson about life. I can still hear him reeling it all off:

In English, the possessive determiner 'its' has no apostrophe before the 's' (e.g. 'the dog wags its tail'), despite possessive nouns being formed in precisely this way (e.g. 'the dog's tail'), and should not be confused with 'it's' which is a contraction of 'it is' (e.g. 'it's my dog') or 'it has'. | *It was while gazing at*

*the sky above the Côte d'Azur that the artist Yves Klein was
inspired to create the purest shade of blue possible: International
Klein Blue. | The mathematical symbol ÷ to signify division
is called an obelus. | In spring 1792, a few months before he
was decapitated, Louis XVI had proposed replacing the straight
blades on guillotines with sloping ones to improve their effi-
cacy. | The longest sentence in Proust's* Remembrance of
Things Past *contains nine hundred and fifty-eight words, the
most famous has eleven ('For a long time I used to go to bed
early.'), the shortest have just one or two (e.g. 'He knocked.'),
and the most beautiful has nine ('We love only what we do
not wholly possess.'). | It was Victor Hugo who introduced the
word 'pieuvre' ('octopus') into the French language when he
used it for the first time in his novel* The Toilers of the Sea. *|
The sum of two consecutive whole numbers equals the difference
of their squares. For example:* $6 + 7 = 13 = 7^2 - 6^2$ . . .

These were moments of pure joy – but a tad solemn too, and
I think everything I learnt on those mornings has remained
etched on my memory. One day – I must have been eleven
– my father informed me, with deep sadness, that he had
passed on more or less everything he knew, and I would
learn the rest from books. At the time, I didn't believe him,
but very soon we began to grow more distant.

My father was haunted by the fear of losing me, of me
being run over by a car, or falling ill, or being kidnapped by
some lunatic when I went to play in the park . . . But ulti-
mately, it was books that drove us apart. And yet these were
books he himself had praised to the skies.

I didn't understand this right away, but books are not
always a route to freedom. Books also lead to separation.

Books not only break walls down, they build them up too. More often than you'd think, they wound, and shatter, and kill. Books may dazzle and shine, but all that glitters is not gold. Much like the pretty face that belonged to Joanna Pawlowski, third runner-up in the Miss Île-de-France competition 2014.

Just before the van crashes, one last memory suddenly rises to the surface. Some mornings, on the way to school, when my father thought we were in danger of being late, we'd break into a run for the last two hundred metres. *You see, Rafa*, he said to me, a few months ago, as he lit one of his cigarettes which he'd smoke right down to the filter, *whenever I think about you, it's always the same image that comes to mind. It's spring, you must be five or six, it's sunny and wet at the same time. We're sprinting through the rain so you won't be late for school. We're running, the two of us, side by side, hand in hand, through droplets of light.*

The light that shone in your eyes.

Your peals of laughter, sparkling and bright.

A life in perfect equilibrium.

12

THE CHANGING FACE
OF THE TRUTH

1.

When Mathilde turned up at Fawles's house, she was armed
with the pump-action shotgun. Her hair was soaking and her
face, devoid of make-up, bore the traces of a sleepless night.
She'd abandoned her little flowery dresses and instead slipped
on a pair of frayed jeans and a quilted parka with a hood.

'The game's up, Nathan!' she blurted out, bursting into
the living room.

Fawles was sitting at the table, in front of Grégoire Audibert's laptop.

'Maybe,' he replied calmly, 'but you're not the only one
making up the rules.'

'Yes, but I was the one who nailed Chapuis's body to the
tree.'

'Why?'

'I had to stage it like that. It needed to be sacrilegious, to
force the authorities to cordon off the island and stop you
escaping.'

'That was a bit pointless. Why would I run away?'

'To avoid me killing you. To avoid your little secrets being revealed to the entire world.'

'When it comes to little secrets, I'd say you're not doing too badly yourself.'

To back up his words, Fawles turned the laptop towards Mathilde, placing her face to face with the photos taken on the night of her brother's birthday.

'Everyone's always believed the Verneuils' daughter was revising for her baccalaureate in Normandy. But that wasn't true. You were there too, at the scene of the tragedy. That must be a weight on your mind, living with a secret like that, mustn't it?'

Mathilde sank down at the end of the table, looking ravaged. Defeated. She placed her weapon on top, within easy reach.

'It's a weight on my mind, but not for the reasons you imagine.'

'Tell me what happened . . .'

'At the beginning of June, while we were revising for the bac exams, I'd gone to stay with my friend Iris at her parents' holiday home in Honfleur, in Normandy. The adults would sometimes come and join us at weekends, but during the week it was just the two of us. We were conscientious and we'd been swotting really hard, so on the morning of 11 June I suggested we take a break.'

'You wanted to go home for your brother's birthday, correct?'

'Yes, I needed to. I'd been aware for several months that Théo had changed. In the past he'd been so happy and full of life, and now he was often sad and anxious, and dark thoughts would run through his mind. I wanted to be there, to show how much I loved him, to make him understand I was there for him if he ever had any problems.'

Mathilde was speaking in a calm, steady voice. Her narrative was carefully structured and you could tell this confession was part of her plan: going in search of the truth, the whole truth, in the deepest recesses of everyone's memory. Including her own.

'Iris told me that if I went back to Paris, she'd take the opportunity to go and spend the day with her cousins, who also lived in Normandy. I let my parents know and asked them not to say anything to Théo so I could give him a surprise. I accompanied Iris in the bus to Le Havre, and then I took the train to Saint-Lazare. It was a sunny day. I walked up the Champs-Élysées, trawling the shops in search of a present for my brother. I was looking for something that would truly make him happy. I ended up buying him the French football team jersey. Then I headed home to the 16th arrondissement by metro, taking Line 9 to La Muette. I arrived around 6 p.m. The apartment was empty. Maman and Théo were on their way back from Sologne, and my father was at the office, as always. I called my mother to suggest she drop by the deli and the pâtissier, to pick up the food and the cake she'd ordered in advance.'

Fawles displayed no emotion. He listened as the young woman ran through her version of that ill-fated night. For twenty years he'd believed he alone held all the keys to the Verneuil affair. He realised now this was far from the case.

'It was a lovely birthday celebration,' Mathilde continued. 'Théo was happy and that's all that mattered to me. Do you have any brothers or sisters, Fawles?'

The writer shook his head.

'I don't know how our relationship would have developed, but at that age Théo adored me and I adored him. I could tell how fragile he was, and I felt as if I'd been entrusted with the mission of keeping him safe. After the match, we celebrated the victory and Théo nodded off on the sofa. Around 11 p.m., I took him, still half asleep, to his bed and tucked him in as I sometimes did before going to my room. I was tired too. I read in bed for a while. In the background I could hear my parents chatting in the kitchen, and then my father calling my grandfather to talk about the football match. I eventually drifted off with *Sentimental Education*.'

Mathilde took a long pause. For a moment, all you could make out was the sound of the rain pelting against the glass and the crackling of logs in the fireplace. It was painful for the young woman to carry on, but this was no time for reticence or procrastination. She narrated the rest almost in a single breath. She was no longer engaged in a conversation, but rather about to plunge into a yawning abyss. One from where it was hard to believe that anyone could emerge unscathed.

2.

'I'd fallen asleep with Flaubert and was woken up by *A Clockwork Orange*. A shot that rattled the entire house. My clock radio showed 23.47. I hadn't been sleeping for very long, but this was the most brutal awakening I had ever experienced. Even though I could sense danger, I dashed out of my room in bare feet. My father's body was in the corridor, lying in a pool of blood. I couldn't bear to look. He had been shot in the face at close range. There was blood and little bits of brain splattered all over the walls. I didn't even have time to scream before a second bullet whistled past my ears, and my mother dropped to the floor in the kitchen doorway. I was way beyond terror. In a zone thick with fear, hovering on the brink of insanity.

'In situations like these, you start losing your mind, and your brain refuses to obey any logic. My immediate reaction was to rush to my room for cover. It took me a couple of seconds to get back inside. I was about to close the door when I realised I'd forgotten Théo. Just as I came out again, another explosion shattered the silence and my brother's body practically fell into my arms. He'd been hit by a bullet fired into his back.

'My survival instinct made me hide under the bed. The room light was off, but the door was still open. Through the doorway I could see my little Théo's dead body. His football jersey was nothing more than one enormous bloodstain.

'I closed my eyes, squeezed my lips and covered my ears. So as not to see, or scream, or hear. I don't know how long I stayed like this, holding my breath. Thirty seconds? Two minutes? Five minutes? When I opened my eyes again, there was a man in my room. From where I was hiding, I could only see his shoes: elasticated brown leather boots. He remained there for a few seconds, without moving, not even looking for me. Evidently, I thought, this meant he didn't know I was in the house. After a short while he turned round and disappeared. I stayed there for several more minutes, in a state of shock, stunned, unable to move. It was the sound of the police siren, the wailing that finally pulled me out of my daze. On my key ring I had the key that opened the hatch leading to the roof. That's how I managed to escape. I can't make any sense of how I reacted. The police turning up should have reassured me, but it had the opposite effect.

'My memory of what happened next is a bit hazier. I think I was acting without really thinking. I walked through the dark to Saint-Lazare and caught the first train back to Normandy. When I arrived in Honfleur, Iris wasn't back yet. When she returned, I somehow found the strength to lie to her. I claimed I'd felt a migraine coming on after leaving her, and hadn't gone to Paris in the end. She believed me, all the more willingly because she could see I looked deathly pale, and insisted on calling a doctor. He arrived mid-morning, just as the cops from Le Havre showed up at the house, accompanied by my grandfather, Patrice Verneuil. He was the one who officially broke the news of the massacre of my family. And that's when my brain short-circuited and I blacked out.

'When I came round, two days later, I couldn't remember a thing about that night. I genuinely thought my parents and Théo had been murdered in my absence. Seen from the outside, it's hard to believe, but nevertheless it's what happened. A genuine case of amnesia which lasted eighteen years. Probably the only solution my subconscious had found to enable me to carry on with my life. Even before the massacre, I'd already been living in a state of permanent anxiety, but the trauma had shut my brain down completely. It was as if my memory had instinctively separated itself from my emotions, in an act of self-preservation. In the years that followed, I was convinced something wasn't quite right. I was weighed down by terrible pain and suffering, which

I blamed – wrongly, to some degree – on the loss of my family. I had, admittedly, suppressed those memories, but they were rotting away inside me, saddling me with an invisible burden.

'It was my grandfather's death, two weeks ago, that ripped apart my veil of ignorance. Just before he died, Patrice Verneuil sent me a large envelope containing a letter outlining his firm belief that, in fact, you were guilty of the murders that had taken place that night. He vented his anger about the cancer that would soon take his life, and prevented him from going and killing you himself. The letter also contained a USB stick with everything saved in one place – the videos of Chapuis and Amrani being interrogated, as well as *all* the photos found on the camera lost off the coast of Hawaii. When I saw images of myself physically there, that dreadful night, my brain suddenly unlocked and the memories came flooding back with all the force of a tidal wave. The past surged over me again in a series of violent flashbacks, a hideous cortege sweeping guilt, and rage, and shame along in its wake. I was drowning, and it seemed it would never end. As if a solid concrete dam had unexpectedly given way, submerging the valley below.

'I could sense my inner defences crumbling: I felt like howling and yelling, I wanted to disappear. I relived that scene, every moment, as though I'd been thrust backwards in time. This was no liberation. It was absolutely terrifying. A mental explosion, which turned my world on its head and plunged me back into the nightmare all over again. I was overwhelmed by images, and sounds, and smells that were so vivid, and so brutal, that it felt a thousand times worse: the deafening burst of gunfire, the splashes of blood, the screams, the bits of brain spattered on the walls, the horror of seeing Théo drop dead right in front of me. What crime had I committed to deserve being put through hell a second time?'

3.

A spurt of urine landed on Ange Agostini. The policeman was unfazed and finished changing his daughter Livia's nappy. He was about to put her back to bed when his mobile rang. It was Jacques Bartoletti, the island's pharmacist, calling to tell him about an accident he'd witnessed. As dawn broke, he'd taken advantage of the lifting of the blockade, and gone out in his boat to fish for amberjack, mackerel and sea bream. But the wind and the rain had forced him to return home earlier than planned. Coming round Le Safranier Point, he'd seen a vehicle skidding off the road and crashing onto the cliffs below. Panic-stricken, Bartoletti had alerted the coastguards immediately. He was now calling for an update.

Ange replied that he didn't know anything about it. After hanging up – and as Livia began spewing up milk, straight onto his T-shirt which already smelt of piss – he made a call to check whether the emergency services on the ground had definitely been informed. But there was no response at the fire station, nor did anyone answer the mobile that belonged to Lieutenant Colonel Benhassi, the man in charge of fire services on the island. Increasingly concerned, Ange decided to head for the scene himself. However, his circumstances were far from ideal. It was his week for looking after the children, and the cards weren't exactly stacking in his favour: for starters, his son Lucca had a throat infection and was tucked up in bed, and in addition the weather was atrocious, which made the roads dangerous.

What a pain . . . Ange went to wake up Lucca as gently as he could, and helped him put on some warm clothes. He then scooped up his son and daughter in his arms – *God, they weigh a ton, these kids* – and left the house via the door that opened into the garage. He helped Lucca climb up into the back of the Piaggio, pulled down the cover and strapped Livia's infant carrier to the passenger seat. Le Safranier Point was only three kilometres from his house, a Provençal villa he'd had built on the plot inherited from his parents, but which Pauline, his ex-wife, found 'too small', 'badly positioned', 'too hemmed in, and gloomy'.

'We'll take it nice and slow, guys.'

In the rear-view mirror, Ange saw his son giving him a thumbs up. The three-wheeler struggled back up the road with hairpin bends that led to the Strada Principale. The surface was very slippery because of the rain, and the Piaggio found it hard going along the steepest sections. Ange's stomach was in knots at the thought of putting his children's lives at risk. He heaved a sigh of relief once they reached the main road. But he wasn't completely out of danger. The storm was lashing Beaumont with a force rarely seen. Ange was always apprehensive on these wild days, when his island, normally so hospitable, flaunted its volatile, malevolent side – as though reflecting the darkness each of us carries within ourselves.

The three-wheeler juddered from side to side, and the rain hammered at the windows. The baby was screaming and, in the back, Lucca's pulse must have been racing. They had just passed Silver Cove Beach when, coming round a bend, they found their way blocked by a large pine branch, snapped off by the storm. Ange stopped on the verge, and motioned to his son to come and sit with his sister in the front while he cleared the road.

The policeman got out into the rain and, with a great deal of effort, managed to shift the branch and the debris obstructing the traffic. He was about to get back into his buggy when he spotted the fire service vehicle fifty metres further on, just before the fork with Botanists' Path. He parked the Piaggio up against the fire engine, told Lucca not to move and ran to join the firemen. Ange was soaking, and in a bit of a sorry state, with water streaming down the neck of his polo shirt and running down his back. He could make out the shell of a car down below, but he wasn't able to identify it.

The tall figure of Najib Benhassi emerged from the mist.

'Hello, Ange.'

The two men shook hands.

'It's the bookseller's van,' said Benhassi, anticipating the question.

'Grégoire Audibert?'

The fireman nodded, and then said:

'He wasn't alone. His employee was in the van with him. A young guy.'

'Raphaël?'

'Raphaël Bataille, that's right,' replied Benhassi, referring to his notes.

He paused and added, pointing to his team:

'We're bringing them up now. They're dead, both of them.'

The poor kid!

Ange was reeling under the blow, caught off guard by death bursting into their lives again just as the blockade's iron grip was beginning to loosen. He exchanged a glance with Benhassi, and noticed the growing look of unease on his face.

'What's on your mind, Najib?'

After a moment's silence, the lieutenant colonel admitted he was baffled:

'There's something really weird. The lad's hands and feet were all tied up.'

'Tied up? With what?'

'With bungee cords. He was tied up with bungee cords.'

4.

The storm was raging. A good minute or so had passed since Mathilde had finished her story. Cocooned in silence, she had the gun pointed menacingly at Fawles once more. The writer was on his feet again. He was standing in front of the huge glazed door, hands behind his back, watching the pines bending and swaying, as if writhing in agony in the torrential rain. After a long pause, he turned round very calmly to face the young woman and said:

'So, if I understand correctly, that's what you think too? That I killed your parents?'

'Apolline was convinced she recognised you, down in the car park. And I could see your shoes clearly, from where I was hiding under the bed. So yes, I think you're a murderer.'

Fawles considered her argument without attempting to

dismiss it. After a moment's thought, he said:

'But what would my motive be?'

'Your motive? You were my mother's lover.'

The writer couldn't mask his surprise.

'That's ridiculous. I've never met your mother!'

'But you wrote her letters. Letters you've managed to get back recently, as it happens.'

Using the barrel of the gun, Mathilde pointed at the pile of correspondence which Fawles had tied up with a ribbon and placed on the table. The writer was quick to retaliate:

'How did you end up with these letters?'

Mathilde delved back into the past again. Still that same night. Still the same sequence of events which, in only a few hours, had turned the lives of so many upside down.

'That evening, 11 June 2000, before we sat down to the birthday dinner, I decided to change into something more suitable. I found a pretty summer dress in my wardrobe, but I didn't have any matching shoes. As I sometimes did, I went to have a rummage through my mother's clothes. She had more than a hundred or so different pairs of shoes. And that's where I came across the letters, in a cardboard box. When I flicked through them, I found myself torn between conflicting emotions. On the one hand, I was shocked to discover my mother had a lover, and on the other, almost despite myself, I was jealous that a man could write her letters that were so poetic, so fiery and full of passion.'

'And you kept the letters for twenty years?'

'I took them to my room so I could read them at leisure, and hid them in my bag. I meant to look through them when I was alone in the house, and put them back afterwards. But I never had the chance. After the tragedy I lost track of them, and I guess I forgot about them too. My paternal grandfather, with whom I lived after the massacre, must have stored them somewhere, along with a number of things that might have reminded me of that evening. But he hadn't forgotten them, and he made the connection with you after hearing Apolline's revelations. He sent them to me along with the USB stick. There's no doubt whatsoever: it's your handwriting, and they're signed with your name.'

'Yes, it was me. I wrote them. But what makes you think they were meant for your mother?'

'They're addressed to someone called S. My mother was called Sofia and they were in her room. That makes a neat little body of evidence, doesn't it?'

Fawles remained silent. Instead, he slid another pawn across the chessboard:

'Why exactly are you here? To kill me?'

'Not straight away. I'd like to give you a present first.'

She dug around in her pocket and pulled out a circular object which she laid flat on the table. Fawles thought at first it was a roll of black sticky tape before realising it was an ink ribbon for a typewriter.

Mathilde walked over to a shelf, picked up the Olivetti and laid it on the table.

'I want a full confession, Fawles.'

'A confession?'

'Before I kill you, I want written proof.'

'Written proof of what?'

'I want everyone to know what you did. I want everyone to know that the great Nathan Fawles is a murderer. You're not going down in history on a pedestal, believe me!'

He stared at the typewriter for a second, looked up at her and spat back:

'Even if I'm a murderer, you can't do anything about my books.'

'Yes, yes, I know, it's all the rage at the moment, wanting to separate the man from the artist: Mr So-and-so has committed all sorts of atrocities, but he's still a brilliant artist. Well, I'm sorry, but it doesn't work that way. Not for me.'

'That's a huge debate. You might be able to kill the artist, but you'll never kill the work of art.'

'I thought your books were overrated.'

'That's not the issue. And deep down inside, you know I'm right.'

'Deep down inside, I feel like putting a couple of bullets in you, Nathan Fawles.'

In a sudden move, she struck him in the small of his back with the butt of the gun to make him sit down.

Fawles collapsed onto the chair, gritting his teeth.

'Do you think it's easy to kill someone? Do you . . . do you think your body of evidence gives you the right to kill me? Just because you feel like it?'

'No, you have the right to a defence, that's true. That's why I'm giving you the chance to be your own lawyer. It's what you liked to say all the time in your interviews: "Ever since I was a teenager, my only weapons have been my old chewed-up Biro and a pad of lined paper." Well, there you go: you've got a typewriter, a ream of paper and half an hour to defend yourself.'

'What do you want, precisely?'

Exasperated, Mathilde held the barrel of the gun to the writer's forehead.

'The truth!' she cried.

Fawles was defiant:

'So you think the truth will let you draw a line under the past, free you from your suffering and allow you to start again from scratch? I hate to tell you, but that's an illusion.'

'Let me be the judge of that.'

'There's no such thing as the truth, Mathilde! Or rather yes, the truth exists, but it's constantly moving, always living and breathing, changing all the time.'

'I've fucking had it with your sophistry, Fawles.'

'Listen, whether you like it or not, the human race isn't some binary thing. We're all evolving in a grey, fluid zone, where even the best among us is always capable of the very worst. Why would you want to put yourself through that? A truth you'll find simply unbearable. Like spraying acid on a fresh wound.'

'I don't need protecting. Not by you, at any rate!' she snapped back.

Then she pointed at the typewriter.

'Go on then, get on with it. Step on it! Give me your version: the bare facts, nothing but the facts. No fancy stuff, no poetry, no digressions, nothing pompous. I'll collect your script in half an hour.'

'No, I'm—'

But another whack from the gun forced him to concede. He grimaced, doubling over as he reeled from the impact. Then he gently slid the ribbon into the machine.

After all, if he had to die today, it might as well be sitting at a typewriter. That was where he belonged. Where he had always felt the least anxious. Saving his skin by lining up some words using a set of little keys: now there was a challenge he was more than capable of taking on.

To warm up, he typed out the first thing that came into his head. A sentence by Georges Simenon, one of his role models, which seemed particularly apt in the circumstances:

```
How different life is when one is living it from when one
picks through it later on!
```

After twenty years, the gentle tapping of the keys under his fingers gave him a thrill. He had missed this, of course, but his absence from the keyboard had not been of his making. Sometimes, even having the will to act isn't enough by itself. It needs a gun to the forehead too.

```
I met Soizic Le Garrec in spring 1996 on a flight from New
York to Paris. She was sitting beside me, by the window,
immersed in one of my novels.
```

Voilà, he was off again . . . He hesitated for a few more seconds, and gave Mathilde one last look as if to say: *there's still time to stop all this, still time to stop me launching a grenade that's about to blow up in our faces and kill us both.*

But there was only one answer in Mathilde's eyes: *go on, chuck your grenade at me, Fawles. Spray me with your acid . . .*

13

MISS SARAJEVO

I met Soizic Le Garrec in spring 1996 on a flight from New York to Paris. She was sitting beside me, by the window, immersed in one of my novels. It was *A Small American Town*, the latest, which she'd bought at the airport. Without introducing myself, I asked her if she liked the book – she'd already read around a hundred pages. And there, up in the midst of the clouds, she replied calmly that she didn't like it all, and simply couldn't understand why everyone was so infatuated with this author. I pointed out that Nathan Fawles had just been awarded the Pulitzer Prize anyway, but she assured me she had no faith in literary prizes, and the bands wrapped around books to trumpet such accolades – which completely ruined their covers – *were merely there to pull in the suckers*. I quoted from Henri Bergson's *Laughter* to impress her ('In short, we do not see the actual things themselves; in most cases we confine ourselves to reading the labels affixed to them'), but she wasn't exactly blown away.

After a short while, unable to contain myself any longer, I revealed that I *was* Nathan Fawles, but that appeared to leave her equally unimpressed. Yet despite this rocky start, we couldn't stop chatting for the six hours of the flight. Or rather, it was I who kept on distracting her from reading with my questions.

Soizic was a young doctor of thirty. I was thirty-two. She told me part of her story in bits and pieces. In 1992, having just finished her studies, she had gone to Bosnia to join her boyfriend at the time, a cameraman for the French TV channel Antenne 2. It was the beginning of what would become the longest siege in modern warfare: the terrible agony of Sarajevo. A few weeks later, her boyfriend had returned to France, or gone off to cover other conflicts elsewhere. Soizic had remained. She had forged a close bond with the humanitarian organisations based out there. For four years she had endured the ordeal of three hundred and fifty thousand inhabitants, placing her skills at the disposal of the besieged city.

I would be quite incapable of giving you a lecture on the subject, but if you really want to gain anything from this account – from my story and, indirectly, your own family's story too – you need to plunge back into the reality of the time: the disintegration of Yugoslavia in the years that followed the fall of the Berlin Wall and the break-up of the USSR. Since the post-war period, the former kingdom of Yugoslavia had been reunified by Marshal Tito thanks to the establishment of a communist federation of six Balkan states: Slovenia, Croatia, Montenegro, Bosnia, Macedonia and Serbia. With the fall of communism, the Balkans witnessed a rise in nationalist movements. In a climate of rising tensions, the most powerful man in the country, Slobodan Milošević, revived the idea of a Greater Serbia, bringing all Serbian minorities together in a single nation. One after the other, Slovenia, Croatia, Bosnia and Macedonia each demanded their independence, triggering a series of violent and murderous conflicts. Against a backdrop of ethnic cleansing and a UN powerless to act, the Bosnian War resulted in carnage with more than a hundred thousand dead.

When I met her, Soizic still bore the mental and physical scars of Sarajevo and its suffering. Four years of terror, constant bombing, hunger and cold. Four years of whistling bullets and surgical operations sometimes performed without anaesthetic. Soizic was one of those people who carry the pain of the whole world deep inside themselves. But all of this had worn her down. The misery of our planet is a burden that can end up crushing you to pieces, if you take it personally.

We landed at around 7 a.m. in the depressing gloom of a grey Roissy. We said goodbye to each other and I took my place in the taxi queue. Everything felt utterly hopeless: the prospect of not seeing her again, the freezing damp that morning, the filthy, polluted clouds which clogged up the sky and seemed to be all that was left on my future horizon. But then an inner force pushed back, prompting me to act. Are you familiar with the Greek concept of *kairos*? It's the decisive moment you mustn't let pass. In every life, even the shittiest, the heavens give you – at least once – a real opportunity to dramatically change your destiny. *Kairos* is the ability to grab hold of that line when life throws it to you. You have to be quick, though. And life doesn't give you a second chance. Well, that morning I knew something crucial was unfolding. I abandoned the queue and retraced my steps. I looked for Soizic all over the terminal and finally found her waiting for the shuttle bus. I told her I'd been invited to go and sign my novels in a bookshop on an island in the Mediterranean. And, without messing around, I suggested she come with me. Since *kairos* can sometimes strike two people at precisely the same moment, Soizic agreed without thinking twice, and we left for the Isle of Beaumont that very day.

We stayed on the island for a fortnight, and fell in love with the place while falling in love with each other at the same time. It was a timeless moment, the kind your bitch of a life will occasionally toss your way to make you believe that happiness really does exist. A necklace of glistening snapshots, gleaming like pearls. In a moment of sheer madness, I sank ten years of royalty payments into The Southern Cross. I could picture us spending happy times there and thought I'd found the ideal place to watch our children grow up. I saw myself writing my future novels there too. I was wrong.

For the next two years, we led the life of a couple in perfect harmony, even if we weren't always together. When we were, we would spend our time in Brittany – where Soizic was from, and where her family lived – and in our hideaway, The Southern Cross. Galvanised by the new love in my life, I had begun writing a new novel called *An Invincible Summer*. The rest of the time, Soizic was out in the field. She had returned to the land that lay close to her heart, the Balkans, and was carrying out projects for the Red Cross.

Sadly, this part of the world hadn't finished with the horror of war. From 1998 onwards, it was Kosovo's turn to go up in flames. Once again, my apologies for having to play the role of history teacher, but it's the only way of ensuring you understand what happened. Kosovo is an autonomous province within Serbia where the majority of the population is Albanian. From the late 1980s onwards, Milošević began to chip away at the autonomy of the province, and then Serbia attempted to recolonise the area by relocating Serbs there.

A section of the Kosovan population was expelled beyond its borders. A resistance movement was formed, initially peacefully through the intervention of its leader Ibrahim Rugova, the 'Gandhi of the Balkans', known for rejecting violence, and then using arms with the creation of the Kosovo Liberation Army – the famed KLA whose support base was located in Albania, where it took advantage of the collapse of the regime to plunder its stock of weapons.

It was during the Kosovo War that Soizic was killed, in the last days of December 1998. According to the report that the Ministry for Foreign Affairs sent her parents, she had been the victim of an ambush while accompanying a British war photographer who was working on a story around thirty kilometres from Pristina. Her body was repatriated to France and buried on 31 December in the little Breton cemetery at Sainte-Marine.

The death of the woman I loved left me devastated. For six months, I shut myself away at home, in a haze of alcohol and prescription drugs. In June 1999, I announced I was giving up writing, as I didn't want anyone to expect anything from me ever again.

The world kept on turning. In spring 1999, after much dithering, the United Nations had finally made up its mind to vote for an intervention in Kosovo which took the form of an aerial bombing campaign. At the start of the summer, Serbian forces pulled out of Kosovo, which became an international protectorate under the mandate of the UN. The war had led to fifteen thousand casualties and thousands of people going missing. A large number of them were civilians. And all of this was happening just two hours from Paris by plane.

When autumn came, I made the decision to go to the Balkans. First to Sarajevo, and then to Kosovo. I wanted to see the places that had mattered to Soizic, where she had spent the last years of her life. The embers of war were still smouldering in the region. I met Kosovans, Bosnians and Serbs. People with a haunted look in their eyes, disorientated people who had spent the previous ten years in fire and chaos, and were trying to rebuild their lives as best they could. I was searching for reminders of Soizic, and I would stumble across her ghostly presence by chance, while walking down a street, or in a garden, or visiting a community clinic. A spirit watching over me, who was my companion in my sorrow. It was heartbreaking, but somehow it made me feel better.

Almost without meaning to, in the random course of conversations I gleaned little nuggets of information from various people who'd met Soizic shortly before she died. A little secret shared over here would lead to a question over there, and so on. Bit by bit, these interconnecting threads wove themselves into a spider's web, transforming my original journey of grief into a detailed inquiry focusing on the circumstances in which Soizic had been killed. I hadn't been back on a mission for a very long time, but I still had my old reflexes and a feel for the region acquired during my stint in humanitarian work. I had a few contacts – and, above all, I had time.

I had always wondered what Soizic was doing in the company of a young journalist from the *Guardian* when she was killed. The guy was called Timothy Mercurio. I had never believed he was a casual lover – and I learnt later on that Mercurio was openly gay. But I never believed the couple just happened to be there either. Soizic spoke Serbo-Croatian. The journalist must have asked her to go with him to interview the locals. I'd heard one particular rumour several times: that Mercurio was investigating the House of the Devil, a former farmstead located in Albania which had been converted into a detention centre and conducted an illegal trade in human organs.

The existence of Kosovan detention centres in Albania wasn't really a scoop. Albania was the support base for the KLA, which had set up prison camps there. But the House of the Devil was another matter. Based on hearsay, this was a place where captives were brought – mostly Serbs, but also Albanians accused of having collaborated with Serbia – in order to sort them according to medical criteria. Following this macabre selection process, some of them would be shot in the head and their organs removed. It was said that this vile trafficking was controlled by men from the Kulshedra, an obscure mafia group which had sown terror throughout the region.

I didn't know what to make of this rumour. To start with, it all seemed quite absurd, and I was aware this was a period that lent itself to wild exaggerations of all kinds intended to discredit one faction or another. But I decided to resume Mercurio and Soizic's investigation from the very beginning, convinced that no one but myself would be able to lead it. At that time, tens of thousands went missing in the former Yugoslavia. Evidence would vanish quickly, and people were afraid to speak. However, I wanted to get to the bottom of the story, and the more I dug into it, the more credible the existence of the House of the Devil appeared to be.

Through my research, I was able to trace some potential witnesses to the trafficking, but they were hardly the most talkative of individuals when it came to getting into the details. Many of those I met were peasant farmers or small-scale artisans, terrified by the men of the Kulshedra. I told you about the kulshedra before, do you remember? It's an evil horned dragon from Albanian folklore. A demonic female monster with nine tongues, silver eyes and a long, deformed body covered in spines and weighed down by two gigantic wings. According to popular belief, a constant supply of human sacrifices is needed to placate this horrific creature – and if its insatiable demands are not met, the kulshedra will spit fire and flame, leaving a trail of fear and bloodshed across the land.

One day, my persistence paid off: I tracked down a driver who had been involved in transporting prisoners to Albania. After endless negotiations, he agreed to drive me to the House of the Devil. It was a disused farm building, isolated deep in the forest, which had fallen into disrepair. I explored every inch of the place in minute detail without finding anything conclusive. It was hard to believe that medical procedures had ever taken place here. The nearest village was ten kilometres away. The local people were hostile. Each time I broached the subject they would clam up, paralysed by the fear of reprisals from the Kulshedra. To avoid speaking to me, they would all pretend they couldn't string two words of English together.

I decided to camp out on site for several days. Finally, a road mender's wife who'd been moved by my story, and had taken pity on me, shared what her husband had told her. The House of the Devil was merely a transit point. A sort of shunting yard where captives were subjected to a whole raft of medical examinations and blood tests. Compatible organ donors were then taken to the Phoenix Clinic, a secret little establishment in the suburbs of Istok in Kosovo.

Thanks to the directions she gave me, I eventually discovered the location of the Phoenix Clinic. In the Kosovo of winter 1999, this was an abandoned, dilapidated building which had been stripped of every last bit of equipment by looters. All that was left was two or three rusty beds, a few broken medical appliances, and bins stuffed with plastic pouches and empty boxes of medication. But the turning point was my encounter with a homeless man squatting on the premises. He was stoned out of his mind, and said his name was Carsten Katz. He was an Austrian anaesthetist who had worked at the clinic when it was still in operation. Later, I discovered he was also known by two rather unflattering names: the Sandman and the Duty Pharmacist.

I questioned him about the clinic, but the man was not in the best of states. He was dripping with sweat, had a wild look in his eyes and was doubled over in pain. Katz was hooked on morphine and prepared to do anything to get his fix. I promised him I'd come back a little later with fresh supplies. I hurried off to Pristina where I spent the rest of the day in search of opiate drugs. I had enough dollars to open the right doors and I made off with all the morphine I could find.

It had been dark for a long time when I returned to the clinic. Carsten Katz looked as terrifying as a zombie. He had turned one of the ventilation ducts into a fireplace and lit a fire with pieces of plywood. When he saw my two phials of morphine, he pounced on me like a lunatic. I gave him his jabs myself and had to wait a long while for him to regain a semblance of calm. Then Katz sat down at the table and told me everything.

Firstly, he confirmed the purpose of the selection procedure at the House of the Devil. Then the fact that certain prisoners were transferred to the Phoenix Clinic. That was where they were executed with a bullet to the brain, before their organs – mainly kidneys – were removed to be transplanted. Unsurprisingly, the recipients were wealthy patients abroad who might pay anything from 50,000 to 100,000 euros per operation. 'The business was well established,' continued Carsten Katz. The anaesthetist claimed he had identified the men involved, who all belonged to the Kulshedra, a little group led by an evil trio. A Kosovan military chief, an Albanian mafioso and a French surgeon: Alexandre Verneuil. While the first two dealt with arresting and transporting captives, it was your father, Mathilde, who supervised the entire 'medical' part. In addition to Katz, your father had recruited a team of doctors: a Turkish surgeon, another from Romania and a Greek head nurse. Guys who knew their stuff in medical terms, but weren't terribly clear when it came to the Hippocratic Oath.

According to Katz, around fifty barbaric operations had been carried out at the Phoenix Clinic. Sometimes the kidneys weren't transplanted on site but dispatched by air to overseas clinics. I grilled the Austrian as much as I possibly could, dangling more vials of morphine in front of him. The Sandman was absolutely positive: Alexandre Verneuil was the real brains behind the business, the one who'd come up with the trafficking system and was steering the whole operation. Worst of all, Kosovo wasn't simply a trial run for your father, but a rehash of a well-oiled trafficking racket he'd already set up elsewhere, in the course of his humanitarian missions. Thanks to his connections and his status, Verneuil had access to databases in several countries, which allowed him to make contact with patients who were seriously ill and prepared to spend a lot of money on a new organ. Of course, all dealings were in cash, or went through offshore bank accounts.

I took two new phials of morphine from my coat pocket. The medic stared at them with a demented gleam in his eyes.

'Now, I'd like you to tell me about Timothy Mercurio.'

'The guy from the *Guardian*?' said Katz. 'He'd been stalking us for several weeks. He'd managed to track back to us through our network, thanks to an informer: a Kosovan nurse who'd worked for us at the start of the operation.'

The Austrian had rolled himself a cigarette and was puffing on it as if his life were at stake.

'The guys from the Kulshedra had threatened Mercurio several times to deter him from carrying on with his investigation, but the journalist wanted to play the hero. One night the guards nabbed him here with his camera. It was totally reckless of him.'

'He wasn't alone.'

'No, he'd come with some blonde who must have been his assistant or an interpreter.'

'Did you kill them?'

'It was Verneuil himself who got rid of them. It was the only option.'

'And the bodies?'

'They were taken somewhere near Pristina, to make it look as though he and the girl had fallen into an ambush. It's all very sad, but I'm not crying over them. Mercurio was well aware of the risks he was taking in coming here.'

You wanted the truth, Mathilde. Well, there you have it: your father wasn't the brilliant, generous doctor he claimed to be. He was a criminal and a murderer. A vile beast who had dozens of deaths on his conscience. And who killed the only woman I've ever loved with his own bare hands.

When I returned to France, I was determined to kill Alexandre Verneuil. But first I took the time to transcribe and record each of the testimonies I'd obtained in the Balkans. I developed and sorted out the many photos I'd taken, edited the footage I'd shot and made detailed inquiries into other theatres of war where your father had inflicted his cruel punishment – all in order to pull together the most comprehensive criminal dossier I could. Not only did I want Verneuil to die, but I also wanted to reveal to the world the monster that he was. In short, exactly what you thought you were doing with me.

Once my case for the prosecution was complete, and when the time came to act, I began to follow him around, spying on him almost everywhere he went. I still didn't know precisely how to go about it. I wanted the torture to last a long time. I wanted him to drain my cup of sorrow to the very last drop. But the more time went on, the more it became glaringly obvious: my revenge was too lenient. By killing Verneuil, I ran the risk of turning him into a victim and bringing his ordeal to an end too quickly. And I wanted to watch him suffer.

On 11 June 2000, I paid a visit to Le Dôme, on Boulevard du Montparnasse, the restaurant where your father was a regular. I left a photocopy of my prosecution file with the maître d', asking him to pass it on to Verneuil. Then I slipped away before he noticed me. I'd made up my mind to contact the authorities and the media the following day, to hand over everything I'd unearthed and all of my evidence. But before that, I wanted Verneuil to be shitting his pants. To have a gnawing fear in the pit of his stomach. I wanted to give him these few extra hours, so he had time to imagine the vice tightening its grip, crushing his bones one by one. A few agonising hours spent fully conscious of his fate, being devoured by anxiety, imagining the tsunami about to come crashing down on him, ripping through his life and the lives of his wife, his children and his parents. Tearing him to shreds.

In the meantime, I returned home, somewhat at a loose

end, and it felt as though Soizic were dying for a second time.

'ZIDANE FOR PRESIDENT! ZIDANE FOR PRESIDENT!'

I was woken shortly before 11 p.m. – I was feeling restless and drenched in sweat – by football fans celebrating the French team's victory. I had spent the afternoon drinking and my mind was a blur. But I was plagued by anxiety. How would someone as demonic as Verneuil react? There was little chance of him sitting there and not doing anything. I had acted without thinking about the repercussions of my actions. Without thinking, in fact, about his wife and two children.

I was seized by a sense of impending horror, and ran out of the house. I picked up my car from the Montalembert parking garage, crossed the Seine and drove to the Jardin du Ranelagh. When I got to Boulevard de Beauséjour, outside the building where your parents lived, I realised at once that something wasn't quite right. The automated shutter at the entrance to the car park was wide open. I drove down the ramp and found a space for my Porsche.

Then everything happened very fast. I was just calling the lift when I heard two shots being fired somewhere upstairs. I dashed into the stairwell and up to the second floor. The door was half open. When I entered the apartment, I was confronted by your father, armed with a pump-action shotgun. The walls and floor in the hallway were streaked with splashes of scarlet. I saw your mother's body, and your brother's was lying at the end of the corridor. And you were next on his list. Like others before him, your father was in the grip of some murderous insanity: he was wiping out his entire family before killing himself. I flung myself onto him to try to disarm him. We struggled with each other on the floor, and suddenly a shot went off, shattering his skull.

And that's how, without knowing it, I saved your life.

14

TWO SURVIVORS FROM THE VOID

1.

Blinding flashes of lightning lit up the room, one after the other, followed swiftly by a rumble of thunder. Mathilde was sitting at the living room table, and was nearing the end of Nathan Fawles's confession. While reading, she'd felt several times that she could no longer breathe, as if the air in the room were getting thinner and she were in danger of having a stroke.

Fawles hadn't confined himself to his narrative. To lend weight to his account, he had taken the evidence from his investigation out of a cupboard. Three thick hardback files to which he had attached the sheaf of typewritten pages.

Mathilde now had proof of her father's shocking brutality right before her eyes. She had demanded the truth, but the truth – the unbearable truth – had left her spinning in confusion. Her heart was thumping so violently it felt as though her arteries were about to burst. Fawles had promised to spray her with acid. Not only had he kept his word, but he'd aimed the jet straight at her eyes.

She could have kicked herself. How could she possibly have been so blind? Neither during her adolescence nor since the death of her parents had she seriously questioned where her family's wealth had come from. Their two-hundred-square-metre home on Boulevard de Beauséjour, the chalet in Val d'Isère, the holiday house in Cap d'Antibes, her father's watch collection, her mother's double-sized walk-in wardrobe – itself as large as a one-bedroom apartment. She was meant to be a journalist. She'd been charged with leading investigations into politicians suspected of misusing corporate assets and prominent figures accused of tax evasion, or the sleazy behaviour of certain company directors, but she'd never bothered to investigate her own self. The age-old story of the pot calling the kettle black.

She could see Fawles through the glazed doors. He'd gone out onto the terrace and was standing completely still. He was staring at the horizon, sheltered from the rain by the wooden slats over the patio. His trusty Bronco was keeping guard close by. Mathilde picked up the gun which she'd placed on the table while she was reading. The gun with the walnut butt and steel barrel, adorned with the terrifying engraving of the kulshedra. The gun that, she now knew, had slaughtered her family.

So what now? wondered Mathilde.

She could simply shoot herself in the head to add the finishing touch. An act which, at that precise moment, felt like it would come as a relief. So often she had been consumed by guilt at not having died along with her brother. Or, equally, she could kill Fawles, and burn his confession and his case file. She had to protect the memory of the Verneuils at any price. A family secret like this is a stain you can never wipe clean. A bomb, which explodes in your face and prevents you having children. An act of pure evil which, as soon as it's out there, is like a virus, infecting your offspring and your descendants for centuries to come. The third solution consisted of killing Fawles and killing herself afterwards, so as to eliminate all witnesses to the whole damn business. To eradicate, once and for all, the deadly plague of the 'Verneuil affair'.

Images of Théo swirled around in her head, refusing to let go. Happy memories. Poignant ones. Her brother's impish face, glowing with kindness. His colourful glasses and that gap between his front teeth. Théo had been so close to her. He'd placed so much trust in his sister. She would often comfort him when he was afraid – of the dark, or monsters in fairy tales, or those little bullies in the playground – and tell him, time and again, not to worry. Reassuring him she'd always be there whenever he needed her. Words that committed her to nothing in the end, because the one time he'd *really* been in danger, she'd been powerless to help. Even worse, she'd only thought about herself, and had fled to her room for safety. She couldn't bear the thought. She would never be able to live with it.

Through the glass, she caught a glimpse of Fawles who, despite the rain, was heading down the stone staircase that led to the pontoon where the Riva was moored. For a split second, she thought he was going to try to escape in the boat, but then she remembered having seen the keys in the little bowl by the front door.

Her ears were buzzing. Her brain was seething and

churning. She found herself slipping from one idea, and one set of emotions, to another. It wasn't strictly true to say she'd never asked herself any questions about her family. From the age of ten – and possibly even earlier – she had constantly switched back and forth, between brighter moments of pure joy and much blacker periods. Times when she was devoured by anxiety and a profound unhappiness without knowing why. Then there had been her eating disorders, which meant she'd twice had to be admitted to the Youth Care Centre.

Now she realised that, even then, the secret of her father's double life had already been festering within her. And it had begun to infect her brother too. An entire chapter of her life suddenly presented itself in a different light: Théo's sad demeanour, his asthma, his harrowing nightmares, his loss of trust in her and his increasingly poor marks at school. The secret had been lurking inside them since childhood, like a poison killing them drop by drop. Beneath the polished veneer of the perfect family, both brother and sister had absorbed the darkness, inhaling a cloud of poisonous fumes. All of this had happened quite unconsciously. Like mind readers, they must have captured things in mid-air: the odd enigmatic word, a certain attitude, things left unsaid, silences that infused them with a vague sense of unease.

And what did her mother really know about her husband's crimes? Not very much, perhaps, but maybe Sofia had accepted things a little too easily, and without probing too deeply into their family's affairs – a world where money flowed like water.

Mathilde could feel herself sinking: in a matter of minutes, she had lost all her points of reference, all the markers that had defined her identity for so long. She was on the verge of turning the gun on herself when – searching desperately for something to cling on to – a detail from Fawles's narrative flashed through her mind. The order in which the bodies had fallen. Suddenly Mathilde began to doubt the writer's version of events. After the trauma of her amnesia, her memories had come flooding back with surprising clarity. And she was convinced her father had been the first to die.

2.

A peal of thunder left the house shuddering, as if it were poised to shear away from the side of the cliff. Armed with the gun, Mathilde walked across the terrace and went down the staircase to join Fawles and his dog near the jetty.

She emerged onto the wide area of stone paving which stretched in front of the lowest level of the house. The writer had taken refuge below the overhang formed by the middle terrace. The building's imposing limestone facade was pierced by a series of opaque portholes, which had intrigued Mathilde the first time she'd seen them. Now she thought this particular section might serve as a boathouse for the Riva, even though a wave or two probably came surging over the pontoon and right up to here on stormy days.

'There's something that doesn't quite square with your story.'

Fawles wearily rubbed the nape of his neck.

'It's the shootings – the order they took place,' said Mathilde. 'You're claiming my father killed my mother first and then my brother, and then he was killed too.'

'That's just what happened.'

'But that's not what I remember at all. When I was woken by the first shot, I ran out of my room and I *saw* my father's body in the corridor. I only saw my mother and my brother being killed *after* that.'

'That's what you *think* you remember. But those are memories you've pieced together.'

'I know what I saw!'

Fawles appeared to be an expert on the subject:

'Memories that resurface several decades after a total blackout might seem to be accurate, but you can't trust them. They're not fundamentally wrong, but they've been corrupted and then put back together.'

'So you're a neurologist now?'

'No, I'm a novelist and I've read about this. A traumatised memory can sometimes be defective, that's pretty obvious. The debate around what's called "false memory syndrome" raged across the US for years. It became known as the "memory wars".'

Mathilde attacked from a different angle:

'The investigation in Kosovo. How come you were the only one leading it?'

'Because I was there, on the ground, but mainly because I never asked anyone's permission.'

'If all this organ trafficking really did happen, it must have left some traces behind. The authorities couldn't sweep something like that under the carpet.'

Fawles gave a hollow laugh.

'You've never been to a war zone, or the Balkans, have you?'

'No, but—'

'There certainly were the beginnings of an investigation,' he said, cutting her short. 'But at the time, the priority was to restore a semblance of the rule of law, not reopen the wounds of the conflict. And moreover, administratively it was a goddamn mess. Between the UN mission, UNMIK, which was then in charge in Kosovo, and the Albanian authorities, everyone was busy passing the buck to each other. It was the same story with the criminal tribunal for the former Yugoslavia, ICTY, and the EU mission in Kosovo, EULEX. Their resources for conducting investigations were extremely limited. I've already explained how complicated it was to pull together enough witness statements, ones that were consistent, and how quickly evidence would disappear in these sorts of matters. Not to mention the language barrier.'

Fawles seemingly had an answer to everything, but Fawles was a writer, and so by nature – Mathilde was sticking to her opinion – a professional liar.

'Why was the shutter open at my parents' apartment that evening, 11 June 2000? At the entrance to the car park?'

Fawles shrugged.

'Karim and Apolline must have forced it open, so they could get upstairs to the retired couple's place. You should have asked your two grandfathers. You know, the torturers.'

'So after you heard the two shots that night, you went rushing up to our apartment?' she asked, forging on with her analysis of Fawles's story.

'Yes, your father had left the door half open.'

'Does that make sense to you?'

'Nothing makes sense to someone who decides to massacre their family!'

'There's still something you're forgetting. The money.'

'What money?'

'You claim that a share of the money that came from organ trafficking was deposited in an offshore account, or maybe several accounts.'

'That's what Carsten Katz told me, yes.'

'So what happened to those accounts? I'm my father's only heir, and I've never heard about them.'

'I guess that's how banking works. It's all very secretive, and there's a lack of transparency in those kinds of organisations.'

'At the time, OK, I'll give you that, but since then we've cleaned things up a bit, when it comes to tax havens.'

'The money's probably lying dormant somewhere, I'd imagine.'

'And Soizic's letters?'

'What about them?'

'What the hell were they doing among my mother's clothes?'

'Your father must have found them on Soizic's body.'

'Fine, but they were incriminating evidence. Why take the risk of hanging on to them?'

Fawles remained unfazed:

'Because they were beautifully written. Because they're a classic of their genre. A masterpiece of epistolary literature.'

'Nothing like modesty.'

'Nothing like the truth.'

'Yes, but why give them to my *mother*, of all people? She hadn't a clue about his double life.'

This time, Fawles was stumped, aware that his version of events was falling to pieces. And Mathilde charged into the breach.

3.

The suicidal storm of self-destruction had blown over. Mathilde was turning back into herself. Or rather, back into the Mathilde she loved. The fiery woman, ablaze with passion. The tough cookie who, ever since childhood, had managed – somehow or other – to overcome so many obstacles. She was still there, full of life, ready for the fight. All that remained was to flush out the enemy.

'I'm not convinced you're telling the truth, Nathan. I'm sure I saw my father's body lying in the corridor before my mother and Théo were killed.'

Now the memory in her head was crystal-clear. Sharp, precise, unshakeable.

The rain had almost stopped. Fawles came out from under his shelter and took a few steps along the pontoon, his hands in his pockets. The terrifying screech of cormorants and sea-gulls filled the air as they circled in the sky.

'Why are you lying to me?' asked Mathilde as she joined him on the jetty.

Fawles looked her straight in the eye. He wasn't beaten. He was resigned.

'You're right. The first shot fired that evening really did kill the person you saw in the corridor. But it wasn't your father.'

'Yes it was!'

He shook his head and narrowed his eyes.

'Your father was far too cautious, and far too meticulous not to have foreseen all that. Given the atrocities he'd committed, he had a feeling that, some day or other, he was in danger of seeing his life being thrown into turmoil. To guard against such a catastrophe, he'd made preparations – just in case he had to make a run for it overnight.'

Mathilde stood rooted to the spot.

'And go where?'

'Alexandre Verneuil was planning to start a new life with a different identity. That's why the offshore accounts weren't in his own name, but someone else's. His alter ego.'

'Who do you mean? Whose body was that in the corridor, Nathan?'

'His name was Dariusz Korbas. He was a Polish man who lived on the streets with his dog. Your father had spotted him a year earlier, on Boulevard du Montparnasse. Dariusz was the same age, and had the same physique. Verneuil had realised at once how useful this man could be to him. He'd struck up a conversation, had met Dariusz again the following day and found him a place in a day centre for the homeless.'

The wind was beginning to change direction, forcing the rain to drizzle out its last few drops.

'Verneuil would often invite Dariusz to eat with him, at the restaurant,' explained Fawles. 'He would pass on clothes he no longer wore, and help him get access to medical treatment. Even your mother saw him several times in her dental surgery, free of charge, without ever suspecting what your father had in mind.'

'But why was he doing all this?'

'So that Dariusz could take his place when Verneuil deemed the time had come to stage his suicide.'

Mathilde felt herself keeling over, as if the wooden pontoon were breaking apart and about to collapse into the sea.

Fawles carried on:

234

'On 11 June 2000, Verneuil asked Dariusz Korbas to drop by and see him just before midnight and to bring his overnight bag, on the pretext he was taking him on board the *Fleuron Saint Jean*.'

'The *Fleuron Saint Jean*?'

'It's a narrowboat moored at the Quai de Javel which has been converted into a hostel, where homeless guys can stay with their dogs. Your father's plan was simple: to kill Korbas before killing the rest of you – your mother, your brother and you. And that's what happened. When Dariusz showed up, your father asked your mother to make him a coffee. He used the time to rifle through Korbas's things. And then, just as they were leaving for the hostel, as Verneuil had pretended they would, he shot him in the face at point-blank range.'

Mathilde objected immediately: she could clearly recall her father's body being identified.

'That's quite true,' said Fawles. 'The body was identified the next day by your grandfather, Patrice Verneuil, and your grandmother. But it was identified amid all the pain and confusion, and more as a pure formality than anything else. They weren't on their guard, and no-one had envisaged such a cunning piece of deception.'

'And the cops?'

'They did a meticulous job: they examined the teeth on the body, and compared the DNA extracted from a comb and a toothbrush found in your father's bathroom.'

'The comb and the brush belonged to Dariusz,' said Mathilde, hazarding a guess.

Fawles nodded:

'That's what the overnight bag was for.'

'But what about his teeth?'

'That was more difficult to get round, but your father had thought of everything: as he and Dariusz were both patients at your mother's surgery, all he'd had to do was switch the two sets of dental X-rays that same afternoon so as to fool the police forensic team.'

'And the letters to Soizic? Why had he put them in my mother's wardrobe?'

'To make the investigators think your mother had a lover. And that Verneuil had carried out the massacre because of his wife's infidelity. The initial "S." supported this theory.'

Fawles shook his hair to get rid of the raindrops. Now the past was returning to plague him in turn, and it was still just as hard to face up to it.

'When I reached the apartment, your father had already killed Dariusz Korbas, your mother and your brother. He had left the door open, that's correct, probably so he could escape more easily. But first he was going to kill you, I know that now. We struggled, I managed to disarm him, and then I whacked him in the face several times with the gun so he couldn't do any more harm. Then I took a look in your room, but I didn't see anyone.'

'That's how I recognised your boots.'

'After that I returned to the living room. Your father was in pretty bad shape, and he was out cold, but he was still alive. I was completely stunned by what I'd just been through. I would only find out much later what had really happened. In the heat of the moment I decided to go back down in the lift, taking Verneuil with me. Once I was in the parking garage, I hauled him into my car, still unconscious, and strapped him into the passenger seat.'

Mathilde now understood why Apolline Chapuis had sworn she'd seen two people in the writer's Porsche.

'I left the building and headed towards the hospital that seemed to be the nearest: Ambroise Paré, in Boulogne-Billancourt. But when I was only a few metres from A&E, I carried straight on without stopping. I drove all night: the Paris ring road, the A6 autoroute, then the A8 as far as Toulon. I couldn't bring myself to have Verneuil treated for his injuries. I couldn't allow him to be the sole survivor from this tragedy. Not when he was entirely to blame.'

4.

'I arrived in Hyères in the early hours of the morning. In the meantime, Verneuil had begun to regain consciousness, but I'd tied him up securely using the straps of the two seat belts.'

Fawles began to speak the way he must have driven that night: fast and without stopping.

'I kept on going, heading for Saint-Julien-les-Roses where my boat was moored. I carried Verneuil onto the Riva, and then I sailed all the way here. I wanted to kill him myself, as I'd meant to do when I'd returned from Kosovo. As I should have done, which would have avoided the carnage I'd just witnessed. But I didn't go through with it straight away. I didn't want him to have a gentle, easy death. I wanted it to be slow, and horrible, and dark.'

Fawles had been walking as he spoke, and was back near the boathouse. Now he seemed to be consumed by a fever:

'To avenge Soizic's murder, and all the others Verneuil had

committed, I felt I had a duty to banish him to hell. But true hell isn't a bullet in your head, or a knife through your heart. True hell is eternal damnation, perpetual suffering, a never-ending cycle of punishment. The myth of Prometheus.'

Mathilde still couldn't see where Fawles was going with all this.

'So I locked Verneuil up. Here, at The Southern Cross,' he continued. 'And after I'd screwed all the answers I needed out of him, I never spoke to him again. I thought I'd be able to satisfy my thirst for revenge in the long run. A revenge to match the pain I had to endure. And the days passed, then weeks, then months, then years. Years of solitude and isolation. Years of punishment and torture which, in the end, led simply to one terrible conclusion: after all this time, the real prisoner wasn't Verneuil. It was me. I'd turned into a jailer whose only captive was myself . . .'

Mathilde was in a daze. She shrank back, reeling from the dreadful truth: Nathan Fawles had kept her father imprisoned in the boathouse for years. In a part of the building hidden away behind opaque portholes. A place no one ever set foot.

She studied the boathouse which merged into the cliff. You could get in through a narrow side entrance or via a large metal roll-up shutter, the kind you'd find on a garage. She glanced at Fawles, looking for confirmation. The writer took a small remote from his pocket and pointed it at the shutter. It began to inch open, grating its way slowly upwards, bit by bit.

5.

The wind rushed into the monster's lair and swirled around, sweeping along with it the repulsive odour of burnt earth, sulphur and urine.

Mathilde summoned up what was left of her strength and determination, and stepped towards the abyss for one final confrontation. She released the safety catch on the gun and clasped the barrel tightly against her body. The wind was lashing against her face, but the cool air somehow felt soothing.

She waited for a long time. She could hear a metallic sound, mixed in with the buffeting of the mistral. The kulshedra's den was shrouded in darkness. The clanking of chains grew louder. And then the demon emerged from the shadows.

Alexandre Verneuil. But no longer in human form. His skin was deathly pale, mottled and shrivelled like a reptile, his shock of white hair formed a terrifying mane, his nails were as long and as sharp as claws, and his face, purplish in colour and covered with pustules, was pierced by two crevasses: a pair of wild eyes which bore the glint of madness.

Mathilde could feel her legs giving way, faced with the creature who had once been her father. In the blink of an eye she became that little girl once more, the child afraid of wolves and ogres. She swallowed hard. Just as she was lowering her weapon, there was a break in the clouds. The fine engravings decorating the barrel sparkled and shimmered in the light. A triumphant kulshedra with silver eyes, its gigantic wings spread wide open. Her body was trembling all over. She held on tightly to the butt of the gun, but—

'Mathilde! I'm scared!'

A familiar lilt. A voice from the land of childhood. A distant memory, lingering somewhere at the back of her mind. Summer 1996. Pine Cove, a few kilometres away. The warm breeze, the cooling shade of conifers, the heady scent of eucalyptus. Théo's peals of laughter. He's seven. He's climbed up, all by himself, to the first ledge on Punta dell'Ago, the little rocky islet that rises from the sea facing the beach. And now he's no longer sure he's brave enough to dive in. A few metres lower down, Mathilde is swimming in turquoise water. She's looking up, craning her neck towards the needle of rock, shouting words of encouragement:

'Go on, Théo! You can do this!'

But her brother is still hesitant. Mathilde waves her arms at him and, with all the conviction she can muster, yells out:

'Trust me!'

The magic words. Words that must never be uttered lightly. Words that mean that, suddenly, Théo's eyes begin to shine and a smile returns to his face. He sprints forward, gathering speed, and plunges into the sea. The image freezes while he's still mid-air, like a pirate poised to attack. A carefree moment, a moment of joy, but one that already embodies its own sense of yearning. A moment cocooned from all that life will later become – the heavy burden of sorrow, and sadness, and pain.

The memory began to grow dim, and finally dissolved into tears.

Mathilde wiped her cheek and edged closer to the dragon. There was nothing evil or frightening about the demon now shivering before her eyes. Not now. A hideous, quivering wreck, a beast with broken wings, dragging itself across the stone paving like a scrawny bag of flesh and bone. A chimera, blinded by the clear light of day.

The mistral was raging around her.

Mathilde was no longer shaking.

She raised the gun to her shoulder.

The ghost of Théo whispered in her ear.

Trust me.

The rain had stopped. The wind had begun to chase the clouds away.

There was only one shot.

A crisp, rapid bang which echoed through the faded sky.

EPILOGUE

'Where do you find inspiration?'

A footnote to

The Secret Life of Writers

BY GUILLAUME MUSSO

Last spring, shortly after the publication of my latest novel, I was invited to take part in a book-signing event at the one and only bookshop on the Isle of Beaumont. Following the death of its previous owner, The Scarlet Rose had just been taken over by a couple of booksellers from Bordeaux. Two young women, brimming with enthusiasm, who were banking on their ability to modernise and resurrect the long-established local business. They were also keen that I should become its patron.

I'd never been to Beaumont before and I didn't know much about its geography. In my mind's eye, the island had become vaguely confused with Porquerolles. However, I accepted the invitation because the new owners were so delightful and friendly, and I knew that Beaumont was where Nathan Fawles, my favourite writer, had lived for almost twenty years.

I had read everywhere that the island's residents were suspicious by nature, and not terribly hospitable, but both my talk and the book-signing that followed were received very warmly indeed, and my conversations with the locals were remarkably pleasant. Everyone had some little anecdote to share, and it felt good to be among them. 'Writers have been welcome on Beaumont since the very beginning,' the two women assured me. They had booked me a charming bed and breakfast for the weekend, located in the west of the island near a convent which was home to a community of Benedictine nuns.

I made the most of these two days to explore every corner of the island, and it wasn't long before I fell in love with this tiny bit of France that wasn't really France at all. A sort of eternal Côte d'Azur, without tourists, bling, pollution or concrete. I couldn't bring myself to leave the island. I decided to extend my stay and began looking for a little house to buy or to rent. That was when I discovered there were no estate agents on Beaumont: a certain percentage of property would be passed on from one family to another, and the rest sold through personal connections. I shared my plans with my landlady, an elderly Irish woman by the name of Colleen Dunbar, who told me about a house that might be available: The Southern Cross, which had belonged to Nathan Fawles. She put me in touch with the person authorised to deal with the sale.

This happened to be Jasper Van Wyck, a legend in the world of New York publishing. One of the last of his kind. Van Wyck had been Fawles's agent, as well as acting for other high-profile authors. He was known, in particular, for having seen *Loreleï Strange* through to publication, when the novel had already been rejected by most publishing houses in Manhattan. Whenever an article about Fawles appeared in the press, it was invariably Van Wyck who was quoted, and I found myself wondering to what extent the two men depended on each other. Even before taking his vow of silence, Fawles had given the impression he hated everyone – journalists, publishers and even his fellow writers too. When I called him, Van Wyck was taking a break in Italy, but he agreed to interrupt his holiday for a day to show me round The Southern Cross.

We arranged to meet, and two days later Jasper came to pick me up at Colleen Dunbar's cottage, driving a rented camouflage-coloured Mini Moke. With his rotund physique and gentle bonhomie, the agent reminded me of Peter Ustinov playing the part of Hercule Poirot: foppish vintage clothes, handlebar moustache, and an impish twinkle in his eyes.

He drove me to Le Safranier Point, and then we ventured inside a vast, wild estate where the scent of the sea breeze mingled with the fragrance of eucalyptus and peppermint. The road twisted and turned up a steep slope, and suddenly the sea appeared along with Fawles's house, a rectangular cuboid in ochre stone, glass and concrete.

I fell under its spell immediately. I'd always dreamt of living in a place like this: a villa clinging to the side of a cliff with blue as far as the eye could see. I imagined children running along the terrace, I pictured my desk facing the sea, where I would write novels with the greatest of ease, as if the beauty of the scenery were an endless source of inspiration.

But Van Wyck was demanding a small fortune, and told me I wasn't the only buyer in the picture. A businessman from the Gulf had already visited several times and put in a firm offer. 'It would be a shame to let this one go,' said Jasper. 'This house was made for a writer to live in.' Although I really had no idea what a writer's house should be like, I was so afraid of it slipping through my fingers that I caved in and spent an insane amount on the purchase.

I moved into The Southern Cross at the end of the summer. The house was in good condition, but needed a serious overhaul. Which was perfect timing, as I felt the need to do something with my hands again. I got onto the job. I would rise at 6 a.m. every morning and write until lunchtime. The afternoons were devoted to renovation work on the villa: painting, plumbing, electricity. Living at The Southern Cross felt slightly intimidating at first. Van Wyck had sold me the house fully furnished, so no matter what I was doing, Fawles's ghost was lurking everywhere: the writer had eaten breakfast at this table, he'd cooked using this oven, drunk his coffee from this very cup. I very quickly became obsessed with Fawles, and wondered if he'd been happy in this house – and why he'd eventually decided to sell it.

Of course, ever since we'd first met, I'd been asking Van Wyck the same question, and despite his affable nature he'd not minced his words in telling me it was none of my business. I'd realised that, were I to broach the subject again, the house would never be mine. I reread Fawles's three novels, downloaded all the articles about him I could find and, more importantly, I talked to people on the island whom he'd met. The islanders painted a rather flattering portrait of the writer. Granted, he was seen as somewhat of a gloomy individual, someone who was wary of tourists and systematically refused to have his picture taken, or to answer questions about his books, but with the locals Fawles was polite and courteous. Far from his image as a surly recluse, he had a great sense of humour, was quite sociable and was a regular at the island's pub, Yeast of Eden. His abrupt departure had taken most people by surprise. Moreover, the circumstances surrounding his decision to leave were not very clear – although it was generally agreed that, the previous autumn, Fawles had suddenly vanished from the local scene after meeting a Swiss journalist who was on holiday on the island. A young woman who had made contact with him when she came to return his dog, a golden retriever called Bronco who'd gone missing for several days. No one really knew much more, and – even if they didn't say it openly – I had a strong feeling the islanders were a little disappointed that he had slipped away without saying goodbye. 'It's writers' shyness,' I said, in his defence. But I don't know whether they believed me.

Winter arrived.

I forged on earnestly, focusing on the renovation of the house in the afternoons and working on my current book in the mornings. To be honest, I wasn't being very productive. I had begun a novel, *Crown Shyness*, which I was struggling to finish. The towering shadow of Nathan Fawles pursued me everywhere. Instead of writing, I would spend the mornings reading up on him. I attempted to track down the Swiss journalist, whose name was Mathilde. Her former colleagues in the newsroom told me, in confidence, that she had handed in her notice, but I couldn't find out any more. I even went as far as tracing her parents in Switzerland, in the canton of Vaud. They responded by saying their daughter was absolutely fine, and told me to bugger off.

In terms of the refurbishment, things were fortunately progressing more quickly. After renovating the main rooms, I began tackling the remoter, lesser-used areas of the house, starting with the boathouse where Fawles must have kept his Riva. Jasper had tried selling it to me, but I wouldn't have known what to do with a boat like that and I'd turned down the opportunity. The boathouse was the only part of the building that I found charged with a negative atmosphere. It was dark and cold. Chillingly cold. To allow the light back in, I restored the elegant oval-shaped windows, which looked like portholes and had previously been bricked up. But I still wasn't satisfied, so I also knocked down several half-walls to make the space feel larger. In one of these walled sections, I was astounded to see some bones emerging from deep inside the concrete.

I instantly began to panic. Were these bones human? When were these walls built? Could Fawles have been mixed up in a murder?

But novelists are inclined to turn anything into a story. That's what they do. I was all too aware of this, and resolved to calm myself down.

A fortnight later, by which time I'd managed to soothe my nerves a little, I made another discovery – this time, in a forgotten corner of the attic. An almond-green Olivetti typewriter, along with a hardback file containing the first hundred pages of what appeared to be an unfinished novel by Fawles.

I was more excited than I had been for a very long time, and came back down to the living room with my precious find tucked under my arm. Night had fallen and the house was freezing. I lit a fire in the suspended hearth which presided over the centre of the room, and helped myself to a glass of Bara No Niwa – Fawles had left two bottles of his favourite whisky in the bar. Then I settled down in the armchair facing the sea to read the typewritten pages. The first time I devoured them hungrily, and then I read them again to savour the words properly.

It was one of the most memorable reading experiences of my life. Quite different to, but just as intense as the feeling I'd had when I first read certain books as a child, or as a teenager – books like *The Three Musketeers*, *Le Grand Meaulnes* or *The Prince of Tides*. These were the opening pages of *An Invincible Summer*, the novel Fawles had been working on before he stopped writing. It was mentioned, notably, in the final interview he'd given to Agence France-Presse. The book promised to be a powerful humanist saga, centred on a cast of characters whom you saw evolving over the four years, or thereabouts, that the siege of Sarajevo had lasted. What I had read of it was merely the first section – a rough draft, still uncorrected and unpolished – but it was a brilliant start, ablaze with talent, easily on a par with anything Fawles had written until then.

In the days that followed, I woke up every morning with a sense of power coursing through my veins, as I kept telling myself I had the privilege of being perhaps the only person in the world to have had access to this manuscript. But once this heady sensation had faded away, I began puzzling over why Fawles had abandoned his narrative mid-flow. The version I'd read was dated October 1998. The novel was well under way by then. Fawles must surely have been happy with his work. Something had to have happened in his life, to make him give up writing so abruptly. A deep depression? A failed relationship? The loss of someone dear? And did this decision have anything to do with the bones I'd found in a wall of the boathouse?

To put my mind at rest, I decided to show them to a specialist. A few years earlier, while doing some research for a thriller, I'd met Fréderique Foucault, a forensic anthropologist who would be called in to examine certain types of crime scene. She suggested I drop by her office, the Paris branch of Inrap, the French institute for preventive archaeological research. So I headed to Rue d'Alésia with a small aluminium case in which I'd assembled a sample of the bones. But at the very last minute, while I was waiting in the reception area, I got cold feet and left. Why in heaven's name was I about to run the risk of tarnishing Fawles's reputation? I was neither a judge nor a journalist. I was a novelist. I was also one of Fawles's readers and, even if it was a bit naive, I was convinced that the author of *Loreleï Strange* and *Les Foudroyés* was neither a bastard nor a murderer.

I got rid of the bones and went to see Jasper Van Wyck in New York, in his little office in the Flatiron District, drowning under a sea of manuscripts. The walls were covered in sepia prints featuring scenes of dragons battling one another, each more monstrous and evil-looking than the last.

'An allegory of the publishing world?' I asked.

'Or the world of writers,' he replied in a flash.

It was a week until Christmas. He was in a good mood,

and invited me to have some oysters with him at the Pearl Oyster Bar on Cornelia Street.

'I hope you're still happy in the house?' he asked. I said I was, but I also told him about my renovation work and the bones I'd found when demolishing a wall inside the boathouse. Jasper was leaning on the bar. He furrowed his brow very slightly, even though the rest of his face remained inscrutable. As he poured me a glass of Sancerre, he told me he was very familiar with the architecture of The Southern Cross. Its construction dated back to the 1950s and '60s, in other words long before Fawles had bought it, and these bones most probably belonged to an animal, such as a cow or sheep, or a dog.

'That's not all I found,' I said, telling him about the hundred pages of *An Invincible Summer*. Initially, Jasper thought I was joking, but then he wasn't so sure. Then I took the first ten pages of the manuscript out of my briefcase. Van Wyck flicked through them and his eyes lit up.

'That son of a bitch! He'd always had me believe he'd burnt the beginning of the novel! What do you want for the rest of it?' he asked.

'Nothing,' I said, handing him the remaining pages, 'I'm not exactly a blackmailer.' He looked at me gratefully, grabbing the hundred-odd pages as if they were a holy relic. As we came out of the oyster bar, I asked him again if he'd had any news from Fawles, but he dodged the question.

I changed the subject by telling him I was in search of a US agent for a new book project: I wanted to tell the story of Nathan Fawles's last days on the Isle of Beaumont, but in the form of a novel.

'That sounds like a really bad idea,' said Jasper, a note of anxiety in his voice.

'It's not a biography, or anything intrusive,' I tried to reassure him, 'it's a piece of fiction, inspired by Fawles. I already have a title: *The Secret Life of Writers*.'

Jasper remained impassive. I hadn't come looking for his blessing, but it bothered me to part company under a cloud.

'I don't want to write about anything else,' I continued. 'For a novelist, there's nothing more painful than carrying a story inside you and not being able to tell it.' This time, Jasper nodded.

'I understand,' he said, before launching into the spiel he normally served up to the press: 'The point about the Nathan Fawles mystery is precisely that there isn't one.'

'Don't worry,' I replied. 'I'll invent something. That's my job.'

Before leaving New York, I bought several ink ribbons from a dealer in Brooklyn who sold second-hand typewriters.

I arrived back at The Southern Cross on a Friday in the early evening, two days before Christmas. It was cold, but as the sun began to dip below the horizon, the view was just as breathtaking as before. Almost unreal. For the first time, I felt as though I had come home.

I placed a record of the original soundtrack to *The Old Gun* on the turntable, struggled to light a fire in the hearth and poured myself a glass of Bara No Niwa. Then I sat down at the living room table in front of the Bakelite Olivetti, and slid one of the ribbons into the machine.

I took a deep breath. It felt good to be back at the keys of a typewriter. That was where I belonged. Where I had always felt the least anxious. To warm up, I typed out the first sentence that came into my head:

> The essential quality in a writer is knowing how to captivate your reader through a good story.

The gentle tapping of the keys under my fingers gave me a little thrill. I carried on:

> Chapter 1.
> Tuesday, 11 September 2018
> The wind was slapping at the sails in a dazzling sky. The dinghy had left the Var coast a little after 1 p.m., and was now flying along at a speed of five knots towards the Isle of Beaumont.

Voilà, I was off again – but no sooner had I put down these first sentences than I was interrupted by a long text message from Jasper Van Wyck. He wanted to let me know, firstly, that he'd be more than happy to read my novel when it was finished. (This was to keep tabs on what I was up to – I wasn't fooled.) He then assured me that Fawles was doing well, and that the writer had asked him to pass on his thanks for having returned those hundred pages, whose existence he claimed to have forgotten. As a mark of his trust in me, Jasper had attached a photo taken the previous week by a tourist in Marrakesh. Laurent Laforêt, who was French and a so-called journalist, had recognised Fawles in the medina and begun snapping away at him. The slimy little hack – having become, in a trice, a paparazzo too – had tried flogging his pictures to a few celebrity websites and magazines, but Jasper had managed to get hold of them before they were published.

Filled with curiosity, I examined the image now displayed on my phone. I recognised the location, as I'd been there when I'd gone to Morocco on holiday: the Souk Haddadine, the district known for its metalworkers and blacksmiths. I remembered it as being a maze of narrow alleys, open to the sky, a dense cluster of little booths and stalls where skilled craftsmen armed with tools and soldering irons were busy hammering, melting down and shaping metal, transforming it into lamps, lanterns, screens and other pieces of wrought-iron furniture.

You could clearly make out three people, surrounded by showers of sparks: Nathan Fawles, the famous Mathilde, and a child, around a year old, sitting in a pushchair.

In the photo, Mathilde was wearing a short jacquard dress, a leather biker jacket and a pair of high-heeled sandals. She had her hand on Fawles's shoulder. Something elusive, something very soft and delicate, yet powerful, as intense as the sun, radiated from her face. Fawles was standing in the foreground, dressed in jeans, a pale-blue linen shirt and a bomber jacket. With his tanned face and limpid, bright eyes, he was still incredibly good-looking. His sunglasses were pushed back on his forehead. You could tell he had spotted the photographer, and was giving him a look that meant something like: *Fuck off, you're never going to hurt us.* His hands were resting on the handlebar of the pushchair. I looked at the child's features and felt slightly unsettled, because he reminded me of myself when I was little. He was blond, with a cute face, a pair of round, colourful glasses and a gap between his front teeth. Despite the invasion of their privacy, the image undeniably captured something: a shared bond, a moment of calm, a life in perfect equilibrium.

Night had fallen at The Southern Cross. I suddenly felt very lonely and a little sad in the midst of the darkness. I got up to turn on the lamps so I could carry on writing.

When I returned to my work table, I took another look at the picture. I'd never met Nathan Fawles, but I felt as though I knew him because I had read and liked his books, and I was living in his home. Every glimmer of light in the photo was absorbed by the toddler's beaming face, and by his bright peals of laughter. And, in an instant, I knew for certain that neither books nor writing had saved Fawles. It was the spark, the twinkle in the child's eyes. That was what the writer had clung on to. His way of getting back on his feet and reconnecting with life.

So I raised my whisky in his direction to clink my glass against his.

I was relieved to know he was happy.

Loreleï
Strange

— ✴ —

Nathan Fawles

For Mathilde

Nathan Fawles

10 March 1998

Ⓛ Ⓑ

Little, Brown and Company
New York Boston London

TRUTH VERSUS FICTION

Where do you find inspiration?

This question always arises, sooner or later, when I meet readers, booksellers or journalists. However, it's not as trite as it might seem. This novel, *The Secret Life of Writers*, offers one possible answer, illustrating the mysterious process that gives birth to a piece of writing. Everything is potentially a source of inspiration and material for a story, but nothing you encounter in a novel is quite as you've seen, or experienced, or come to know it in real life. Just like a strange dream, little details from the real world can turn up there, but distorted in some way, and become a core part of the narrative as it slowly takes shape. And so those elements enter the realm of fiction. Still true, but no longer real.

For example, the camera that leads Mathilde to believe she's unmasked a murderer was sparked by a little item in the news. A Canon PowerShot was discovered on a beach in Taiwan, having drifted for six years across the ocean from Hawaii. The real one contained nothing more than holiday snaps. The camera in the novel, however, holds something much more dangerous . . .

Another example: the 'angel with golden hair', the title of the second part of the novel, is the affectionate name Vladimir Nabokov gave to his beloved wife Vera in one of the countless letters he wrote to her. I was thinking about the beauty of those letters, as well as the deeply moving exchanges between Albert Camus and Maria Casarès, when I penned the correspondence between S. and Nathan Fawles.

As for the Isle of Beaumont, this fictional island is inspired partly by the astonishing town of Atherton, in California, and partly by (the far more appealing) Porquerolles, a Mediterranean island off the French coast, as well as my travels to Hydra, Corsica and the Isle of Skye.

The bookseller, Grégoire Audibert, owes much of his disenchantment to Philip Roth, and to Roth's pessimism regarding the future of reading.

And finally, there's Nathan Fawles. It's been a pleasure to walk by his side through these pages: this man who yearns for seclusion, who's given up writing and retreated from the media spotlight, who's prone to surly preening and posturing. He borrows these traits from here and there – some from Milan Kundera and J.D. Salinger, others from Philip Roth (yes, him again) and Elena Ferrante . . . But it does feel, now, as though he exists in his own right, and – like the epilogue's fictional Guillaume Musso – I would be delighted to learn that he'd rediscovered his zest for life, in some other corner of the world.

READ AN EXTRACT FROM

THE REUNION

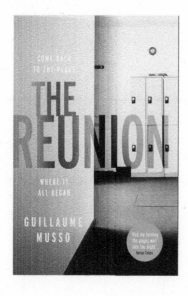

'Extraordinary'
Sunday Times

'Breathtakingly good'
Daily Mail

'One of the great thriller writers of our age'
Daily Express

2017

Southernmost point, Cap d'Antibes, May 13

Manon Agostini parked her patrol car at the end of the Chemin de la Garoupe. She slammed the door of the battered old Renault Kangoo, inwardly railing at the chain of events that had led her here.

At about 9 p.m., a security guard at one the most opulent mansions on the cape had called the *commissariat* in Antibes to report hearing a firecracker or possibly a gunshot – some strange noise – coming from the rocky coastal path. The Antibes *commissariat* attached little importance to the call, and relayed the information on to the local police station, who could think of nothing better to do than radio *her*, even though she was not on duty.

At the point when her superior officer called to ask her to check out the coast road, Manon was already in evening dress and preparing to go out. She wanted to tell him to fuck off, but she felt she could not say no to him. Just that morning, he had given her permission to use the Kangoo outside working hours. Manon's own car had recently died a death, and she desperately needed a car that Saturday night to attend an event that was important to her.

The school she had attended, the Lycée International Saint-Exupéry, was celebrating its fiftieth anniversary and there was to be a reunion of her former classmates. Manon secretly hoped she might run into a guy she had been smitten with long ago. A boy who was not like the others, but whom she had stupidly passed over at the time, preferring to date older guys who had all turned out to be utter shits. There was nothing rational about her hope – she could not be sure that he would be there, and besides, he had probably forgotten that she ever existed – but she needed to believe that *something* was finally going to happen in her life. Manicure, haircut, clothes shopping: Manon had spent all afternoon getting ready. She had blown three hundred euros on a designer dress – midnight-blue lace with a silk bodice – borrowed a pearl choker from her sister and a pair of slingbacks from her best friend – Stuart Weitzman suede pumps that pinched her feet.

Tottering on her high heels, Manon flicked on her phone's flashlight setting and headed down the narrow trail that hugged the coast as far as the Villa Eilenroc. She knew the area like the back of her hand; as a child, her father used to take her here to fish in the streams. Locals used to call this area Smugglers' Way; later it appeared in guidebooks under the intriguing moniker of Sentier de Tire-Poil – Hair-Pluck Lane. These days, it was known by the prosaic, anodyne name of 'the coastal path'.

After some fifty metres, Manon came to a barrier with a hazard warning sign: 'Danger – No Entry'. Earlier in the week, a fierce storm had lashed the coast, and the waves had caused landslides that had cut off certain sections of the path.

Manon hesitated for a moment, then scrambled over the barrier.

1992

Southernmost point, Cap d'Antibes, October 1

Vinca Rockwell blithely hopped and skipped as she passed
the beach of La Joliette. It was 10 p.m. To get here from
the lycée, she had had to sweet-talk a friend from her class
who owned a moped to drive her as far as the Chemin de la
Garoupe.

As she set off down Smugglers' Way, she could feel but-
terflies fluttering in the pit of her stomach. She was going to
meet Alexis. She was going to meet the love of her life!

A fierce gale was blowing, but the night was so beautiful,
the sky so cloudless, she could see almost as well as in daylight.
Vinca had always loved this place, because it was so wild, so
unlike the clichéd image of summer on the French Riviera.
When the sun shone, you were dazzled by the tawny-white
glare of the limestone crags, the myriad shades of blue that
bathed the narrow inlets. Once, while gazing out towards
the Lérins islands, she had seen a pod of dolphins.

On nights like tonight, when the wind howled, it was a
very different place. The sheer rockface loomed dangerously;

268

the olives and the pine trees seemed to writhe in pain, as though trying to uproot themselves. Vinca did not care. She was going to meet Alexis. She was going to meet the love of her life!

2017

Fuck's sake!

The heel of one of Manon's pumps had snapped off. *Jesus.* She'd now have to stop off at her apartment before she went to the reunion, and the friend who'd lent her these shoes would let rip at her tomorrow. She slipped them off, shoved them into her bag and carried on barefoot.

She was still following the narrow, paved path that overlooked the cliffs. The air was pure and invigorating. The mistral had swept the night sky of clouds and scattered it with constellations.

The view was breathtaking, sweeping from the old city walls of Antibes across the bay of Nice, framed by the mountains inland. Here, in the shelter of the pine forests, were some of the most lavish properties on the Côte d'Azur. The air quivered with the crash of waves sending up sea spray; she could feel the brute force of the sea.

The area had seen many tragic accidents in the past. The swell from roiling waves had swept away fishermen, tourists, even couples who had come to make love by the shores. The resulting outcry had forced the authorities to secure the way, building concrete steps, clearing the path and erecting barriers to thwart the hikers' impulse to get too close to the edge. But it took only a few hours of high winds to turn it into dangerous terrain once more.

Manon had just reached a spot where a fallen Aleppo pine had buckled the barrier and blocked the path. Impossible to go any farther. She considered turning back. There was not a living soul around – the gale-force mistral had kept people away.

Get the hell out, girl.

She stood motionless and listened to the wind blowing. It was like a plaintive howl, at once close and distant. A muted threat.

Although she was barefoot, she leapt up onto a boulder, skirted the obstruction, and walked on, with only her phone to light the way.

A dark figure was silhouetted some way down the cliff face. She peered into the gloom. No, she was too far away to make out what it was. With great care, she tried to climb down. She heard a tearing sound. The hem of her lace dress had ripped, but she ignored it. Now she could see the figure that had caught her eye. It was a body. The corpse of a woman sprawled on the rocks. As she moved closer, she felt terror grip her. This was no accident. The woman's face had been beaten to a bloody pulp. *God Almighty.* Manon felt her legs give way under her, and knew she was about to collapse. She keyed the security code into her phone to call for help. There was no signal, but still the screen said: *Emergency calls only.* She was about to press CALL when she realised that she was not alone. A little further away, a man sat, sobbing. Slumped on the ground, he wept, his face buried in his hands.

Manon was terrified. In that moment, she regretted coming out unarmed. Warily, she approached him. The man sat up and, when he raised his head, Manon recognised him.

'It was me . . . This is my fault . . .' he said, pointing at the corpse.

1992

Lithe and graceful, Vinca Rockwell bounded over the rocks. The wind was blustering more fiercely. But Vinca revelled in it. The swell, the danger, the heady sea air, the steep crags. Nothing in her life had ever been as intoxicating as meeting Alexis. A profound, all-consuming magnetism. A meeting of minds and bodies. If she lived to be a hundred, nothing would ever compare to that memory. The prospect of meeting with Alexis in secret, of making love in some rocky crevice, was exhilarating.

She could feel the warm wind envelop her, whipping around her legs, lifting her skirt like a prologue to the long-awaited embrace. Her heart was beginning to race, the wave of heat coursing through her, the pulse of blood, a throbbing that made every inch of her body quiver.

She was going to meet Alexis, she was going to meet the love of her life!

Alexis was this thunderstorm, this night, this moment. Deep down, Vinca knew she was making a mistake, knew that things would end badly. But she would not have traded the thrill of this moment for anything in the world. The anticipation, the wild madness of love, the painful pleasure of being engulfed by the night.

'Vinca!'

Suddenly, the figure of Alexis was silhouetted against the clear, moonlit sky. Vinca stepped forward to greet the shadow. In the blink of an eye, Vinca could almost feel the pleasures that were to come. Intense, burning, overpowering. Bodies melding and dissolving until they became one with the wind, the waves. Cries mingling with those of the gulls. The tremor, the overwhelming blast, the blinding flash that trills through the body and makes if feel as though one's whole being has shattered into a thousand pieces.

'Alexis!'

As Vinca finally embraced her lover, she heard the voice again, whispering that this would not end well. But the girl cared nothing for the future. Love is everything, or it is nothing.

All that mattered was *now*.

The blazing, baleful beauty of the night.